GER
T a   her

33692

STOCKTON
Township Public Library
Stockton, IL

Books may be drawn for two weeks and renewed once.

A fine of five cents a library day shall be paid for each book kept overtime.

Borrower's card must be presented whenever a book is taken. If card is lost a new one will be given for payment of 25 cents.

Each borrower must pay for damage to books.

KEEP YOUR CARD IN THIS POCKET

DEMCO

TACKETT
AND THE TEACHER

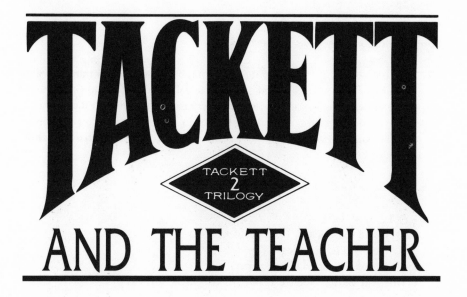

TACKETT

TACKETT
2
TRILOGY

AND THE TEACHER

LYN NOFZIGER

TUMBLEWEED PRESS
Washington, D.C.

Library of Congress Cataloging-in-Publication Data

Nofziger, Franklyn C.
    Tackett and the teacher/Lyn Nofziger.
       p. cm.—(Tackett trilogy : 2)
    ISBN 0-89528-488-9 (acid-free paper)
    I. Title. II. Series: Nofziger, Franklyn C.   Tackett trilogy :
2.
    PS3564.O34T33   1993 vol. 2
    813'.54—dc20
                                            93-45949
                                             CIP

Published in the United States by
Tumbleweed Press
an imprint of Regnery Publishing, Inc.
422 First St., SE
Washington, DC 20003

Distributed to the trade by
National Book Network
4720-A Boston Way
Lanham, MD 20706

Printed on acid-free paper.

Manufactured in the United States of America.

10 9 8 7 6 5 4 3 2 1

In Memory of Frank Tarry
A good husband, a good father, a good friend

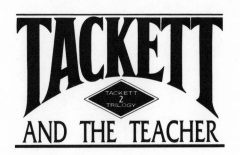

TACKETT

TACKETT 2 TRILOGY

AND THE TEACHER

CHAPTER 1

I RODE INTO ABILENE on a hot Texas day in early September. I was looking for the schoolhouse, or, more accurately, I was looking for a young woman who was supposed to be teaching there. Since it wasn't at the end of town I rode in at, I trotted on through, taking in the saloons—three, the jail—one, the restaurants—two, the church—one, the hotel—one, and sundry business establishments. That was this side of the tracks. Later on I might consider checking out the other side. There'd be more saloons there, a few cribs, and a kind of shantytown. And the toughs and the loafers and the cowboys looking for a wild time.

The schoolhouse was the last building on the outskirts of town. Class had just let out and kids of all ages were scattering for home. Some of the farm and ranch kids were on horseback while the townies were on foot.

I swung down from Old Dobbin, a bay gelding I'd won in a poker game a while back from a good rancher but poor stud player named Shea, and tied him to a hitching post. I discovered that by now Abilene was big enough so it had a two-room schoolhouse with the rooms separated by a hallway where the pupils hung their coats and sweaters.

I headed for the door on my right, but stopped when I heard voices coming from inside the room. The first voice was a woman's.

"I tell you I don't know where she is. She didn't come in today."

A gruff man's voice retorted, "I think you're lying."

"I resent that, sir. Now please leave. I have work to do," the woman's voice said.

"Don't get high and mighty with me," the man rasped, "or I'll . . ."

"Take your hands off of me! Ohhhh!" The woman's voice rose in pain.

I busted in.

A big man with black hair and wearing a black suit had a slim, fragile-looking woman by both arms. He was starting to shake her when I said, "Let her go, Mister."

He dropped his hands and swung toward me. Ordinarily he might have been handsome in a coarse sort of way but now his face was contorted in anger.

"Butt out, friend," he snarled. "This is a private matter."

"Not now it ain't," I said.

He took a threatening step toward me, but I wasn't in any mood to argue so I fetched my six-gun from its holster and pointed it at him.

"Whyn't you leave," I suggested, motioning him toward the door with the barrel of my gun.

I stepped aside to let him pass. He glared at me, then headed for the door.

"You're messing in where you don't belong, stranger," he said.

To the woman he said, "I'll be back. And I'll find out what I want to know."

"Lay a hand on her, Mister, and I'll see you run out of town on a rail," I said.

He gave a nasty laugh. "You have the wrong man and the wrong town," he said, walking out the door.

"Oh, dear," the woman said. "I think I've gotten you in trouble."

"I been there before," I said.

"That doesn't surprise me at all," she said with a slight smile, all the time eyeing me carefully.

What she saw wasn't much. I'm big enough, all right, standing, as I do, over six feet two in my boots and weighing right around 200 pounds with most of my weight in my shoulders and arms. But I never was a raving beauty and a three-inch knife scar on my left cheek and a white patch of hair on the right side of my head doesn't help any.

I got the scar from a Mexican down in El Paso who was quicker with a knife than I thought he'd be and the patch of white hair had come from a rifle bullet that burrowed along the side of my head before I was able to duck. My otherwise brown hair was shaggy from not having been cut for three months. I had a two-day stubble of beard and I was dusty from half a day on the trail.

I'd been drifting over a three-month period from Nora, a little town on the Arizona-New Mexico border, about 600 miles due west, and my clothes showed it. Abilene, I'd figured, would be a good place to rest and get cleaned up and get some new duds.

But first, there was something I had to do; it was the reason I'd come to Abilene in the first place. There was a schoolteacher here named Elizabeth Doyle and I wanted to talk to her about her pa, old Billy Bob Doyle, who'd been a friend of mine back at the R Bar R, a ranch outside of Nora. Billy Bob had been killed by rustlers. In turn I'd killed the man who shot him.

Billy Bob had been carrying a letter from his daughter which is how I knew about her and I figured she had a right to know how her pa had died as well as how he'd lived. He'd been a fine man. He'd lost an arm as a result of a gunshot wound, but he'd never took a back seat to no man. I wanted her to know that.

There was another reason I wanted to see her, too, but I wasn't talking about that. It had to do with Ma. She'd died a few months back and about the only thing she left me was a diary. She'd never talked about my pa, who I never knew, or where we'd come from or anything like that, and I thought maybe the diary would tell me some things I wanted to know. Trouble was, I couldn't read hardly at all, just a few simple printed words but not any handwriting. I could sign my name but that was about it.

Even the letter from Liddy Doyle to her pa I'd had to have one of the hands read it to me. Now I thought maybe if I got friendly with her she might teach me to read.

Back at the R Bar R there was a girl named Esme who'd offered to teach me but I wasn't comfortable with that. Besides, I was hoping to go back some day and surprise her by showing her I could read and write. Maybe then I could think seriously about her marrying me.

"Beggin' yer pardon, ma'am, but I'm lookin' for a lady school-marm named Elizabeth Doyle. Might you be able to help me?" I asked.

"Oh, dear," the woman said. "You're the second person to ask about Liddy—Elizabeth—we call her Liddy. That terrible man who was just here, Mr. Giucy, was asking for her. I told him I didn't know where she was. Today is the first day of school and she was supposed to be here, but she never showed up. If she doesn't come tomorrow they'll have to find another teacher. We have too many children for just one to handle."

"Do ya know where she lives, or where I might begin lookin' for her?" I asked.

"I'm sorry, sir," she said. "While you were very nice to help me a few minutes ago, I don't know you and if Liddy's in some sort of trouble I don't want to make things more difficult for her."

"Look, Miss—uhh?"

"Venn. Ada Venn."

"Look, Miss Venn," I said. "My name is Tackett. Del Tackett—William Delligan Tackett, if you want it all. I don't know Miss Doyle. Never met her. But I rode with her pa. And I helped bury him. He was my friend. And I thought mebbe I ought to tell her about him."

"Oh, dear," she said. "I'm so sorry. Of course I'll do what I can to help you find her. She boards with Mrs. Jenkins, a few minutes' walk from here. If you'd like I'll take you there."

"If you'd just give me directions, ma'am, I'll find it."

"We pass my house on the way," she said. "I wonder if I might impose on you to escort me there. That awful Mr. Giucy has made me a little bit uneasy."

"Be glad to, ma'am," I said. "Just who is that feller anyway? And what gives him the right to come around and try to manhandle you?"

"His name is Crispen Giucy and he owns several businesses here in town," she said. "The general store and a place called Crispen Giucy Saloon and Dance Hall are two that I know of. We have a city council here now and he's a member of it. Some people think that some of the gambling that goes on at the saloon isn't honest and they think some of the dance hall girls are, well, more than that."

By this time she'd gathered up some papers and we were headed out the door. I untied Old Dobbin and we started walking toward town. She was a good walker, and I didn't have to slow down none to let her keep up.

At second look she wasn't as fragile as I'd thought; she'd just seemed that way next to the hulking Crispen Giucy. She couldn't have been much over thirty, but her hair, a light brown and done up in a bun, was beginning to show strands of gray. She was tall and slender but you'd never mistake her for a boy. She had blue eyes, a straight nose, and full lips. Not a bad-looking woman, I thought, sneaking a glance at her now and then as we walked.

A hundred yards from the school was a livery stable and beyond it a blacksmith shop. At the smithy the road forked off to the left, the main road continuing through the heart of town and the fork curving behind town and running parallel to the main road. We took the fork, alongside of which were a number of houses. The second one we came to belonged to Ada Venn.

It was a small wooden cottage, painted white, and surrounded by a picket fence. A middle-sized, short-haired mutt, white with spots of black on him, rose from where he was lying on the porch, stretched, and moseyed down the pathway as Ada Venn unlatched the gate. He gave a halfhearted bark at me, but then turned to his mistress and wagged his tail as she patted his head.

"Thank you so much for seeing me home," she said. "Won't you come in for a bit and have a cup of coffee or tea? You look as if you could use one."

"I surely could, ma'am," I said. "That's mighty kind of you."

There was a hitching post outside the fence and I tied Old Dobbin to it and followed her into the house. It was small inside, too, with a sitting room or parlor, a kitchen with a tiny dining room off of it, and either a large bedroom or two smaller ones. She took me into the kitchen where she dipped some water from a large kettle into a basin and handed me a bar of soap and a towel.

"You may wash up if you like," she said. "Make yourself at home and I will be out in a minute."

I washed my face and hands and combed my hair with my fingers, using a mirror hanging over the sink. I wandered into the parlor and looked around. There was a sofa, an easy chair, and two straight-backed chairs. A small piano sat against one wall and there was a picture on it of a man and woman who likely were her father and mother.

In a few minutes Ada Venn entered the room followed by another woman, somewhat younger, somewhat prettier, with facial features that reminded me of Billy Bob Doyle. She had circles under her eyes and a worried look on her face.

"Mr. Tackett," Ada Venn said, "this is Elizabeth Doyle. I wasn't aware that she was here. I've told her that you wanted to see her and that she has nothing to fear from you.

"Liddy, this is Mr. Tackett, the man who rescued me from Mr. Giucy."

Liddy Doyle extended a long, slim hand and I taken it and shook it gently.

"Miss Doyle," I said. "I'm mighty glad to see you. I come a long way just to talk to you."

Ada Venn said, "You two sit down and get acquainted. I'll go make some coffee."

She left the room and Liddy Doyle seated herself on the sofa and I taken one of the straight-backed chairs. She was a pretty girl all right, slender, like Ada Venn, with red hair, unusually bright green eyes, and a pale complexion. She was tall for a woman, maybe five feet six. She gave me a wan smile.

"I suppose you're wondering what this is all about," she said. "I certainly am sorry. Mr. Giucy is my problem and I didn't mean to inflict him on you and Ada."

"Miss Doyle," I said, "I come here to tell you about your daddy because he was a friend of mine. And I aim to do that. I didn't come here to mix into your affairs."

"I understand," she said.

"Howsomever," I added, "as I say, your pa was a friend of mine and that makes you my friend, too. So if you want some help all you got to do is ask. And if that means whompin' Mr. Crispen Giucy why so be it."

A look of alarm spread across her pale face. "Oh, no. You mustn't get involved. Crispen Giucy is a dangerous man and he has a great deal of influence in Abilene."

She changed the subject quickly. "It was very nice of you to come all this way to tell me about Father. You know, I received a very nice letter from the lady he worked for, Miss Esmeralda

Rankin, I believe her name is. She also sent along his things. There wasn't very much, a few letters, mostly from me, an old tally book, and some odds and ends. But I'm so grateful that you came. There is nothing like talking to someone who knew him."

Just then Ada Venn came in with a tray on which was a pot of coffee, three china cups and saucers, and a plateful of cookies. I taken a sip of the coffee. It was hot and strong and it tasted good. I picked up a cookie, meaning to dunk it in the coffee, but I looked at those ladies holding their cups with their little fingers sticking out and thought better of it.

I wasn't no gentleman, being raised as I was in the goldfields of the Sierra Nevada Mountains where Ma scratched out a living panning for gold. From everything I could remember about her she'd had a good upbringing, but after working from can see to can't see seven days a week most of the time, she just never got around to teaching me manners or even teaching me to do much more than write my name. And I wasn't even very good at that.

But I'd been riding alone since I was sixteen and you learn to be observing when you're out there alone and your life may depend on it. So I noticed little things, such as the way these ladies drank their coffee and ate their cookies, and I tried to imitate them, all but sticking out my little finger; I wasn't about to do that.

So instead of dunking my cookie I nibbled at it. Ada Venn looked at me and laughed a friendly laugh.

"There are lots of cookies, Mr. Tackett. Please help yourself. You said you've been riding most of the day and you must be hungry."

I put the rest of the cookie in my mouth and latched onto another. For a few minutes there we didn't do much talking whilst I cleaned up the plate of cookies and swallowed a second cup of coffee.

After that Ada Venn excused herself, saying she had lessons to prepare for tomorrow, and left Elizabeth Doyle—"Please call me Liddy," she said—and me to talk.

I told her of how I'd known of her pa when he was a Texas Ranger and how I'd run into him back there in that little town of Nora and how he'd talked me into going to work for Esmeralda Rankin at the R Bar R ranch.

And I told her how he'd been killed by a man he thought was a friend and how I'd killed that man in a gunfight up in a rustler hideout in the mountains. She blinked back tears when I told her how her pa had died and I could see a glint of satisfaction in her green eyes when she heard how I'd avenged him.

In turn she told me a lot I hadn't known about old Billy Bob. He'd had a small ranch in East Texas when Liddy was born. But after a few years rustlers and drouth had put him out of business and he and his wife and daughter had moved into town where he'd taken a job as a deputy marshal. A year later her mother had taken ill and died and Billy Bob had sent her to live with his sister over in Tyler. About the same time he'd signed on as a Texas Ranger. She'd spent most of her childhood in Tyler, and once in a while for the first few years her father would come by and see her.

Then an infected bullet wound had cost him his arm and his job. Despondent, he'd taken to drinking heavily for several years. By the time he'd gotten control of himself he'd drifted over into the Arizona-New Mexico country and eventually had latched onto a job at the R Bar R.

He'd written Liddy a long letter telling her where he was and that he'd finally straightened himself out. After that they'd stayed in touch. By this time she was grown and had taught a year in Abilene. She'd been planning to visit Billy Bob when word had come that he'd been killed.

"I don't know what I'm going to do now," she said. "Maybe I'll go back to Tyler. I had planned to teach here at least this year, but I'm afraid that's not possible now." She sighed and gave me a forlorn look.

"Crispen Giucy?" I asked.

She nodded. "He wants to marry me, but I can't stand him. He thinks that just because he's rich and successful any girl would be lucky to have him. But—ugh—he's greasy and overbearing and arrogant and—and just not nice."

"Have you told him yer not interested?"

"Yes, but he won't take no for an answer. Yesterday he told me if I didn't marry him I'd be sorry. He frightened me. That's why I didn't show up at school today. I just don't know what to do."

Just then Ada Venn came into the room. "Pardon me for intruding," she said. "I didn't mean to eavesdrop but I heard what Liddy said just now. Liddy, why don't you get your things from Mrs. Jenkins and come spend the night with me? Maybe things will look different in the morning. Besides, I would feel better if I were not alone."

"That's very kind of you, Ada," Liddy said. "If you're certain I would not be in the way."

"Of course not, my dear."

"Mr. Tackett," Ada Venn turned to me, "I know this is a terrible imposition but I wonder if I could ask you to go with Liddy. I know she would feel safer. And when you come back perhaps I could persuade you to stay for dinner."

"Miss Venn . . . ," I said.

"Ada," she said. "Since we've become friends."

"And call me Liddy," Elizabeth Doyle repeated.

"Ada," I amended, "I'll be pleased to go with Liddy. And I'd be plumb delighted to stay for dinner, especially if there's more of them cookies."

Mrs. Jenkins' house was at the other end of Abilene, about a ten-minute walk from Ada's. I left Old Dobbin hitched in front of Ada's house and we set out walking to Mrs. Jenkins' place. I was tired from my days in the saddle, but walking down the road with a pretty girl made me forget my tiredness. This was twice today that

I'd had a chance to walk with a good-looking woman and that was two more chances than I'd had in the last three months.

As we turned to walk up the path to Mrs. Jenkins' house I noticed right off that something wasn't right. The front door was wide open. I pushed ahead of Liddy and strode through the doorway, my hand on the butt of my gun.

But the only person in the entry hall was an elderly, gray-haired woman who was sitting on the floor, half reclining against the wall. She was holding her jaw and moaning softly.

At my shoulder I heard Liddy gasp and say, "Mrs. Jenkins! Are you all right?"

Mrs. Jenkins looked up at us and burst into tears.

In a second Liddy was on her knees beside her, with her arms around her. After a minute or so the sobbing stopped and Liddy stood up.

"Help me get her into her bedroom," she said.

"No, no, the parlor will be all right," Mrs. Jenkins said, holding her jaw again.

She was a stout woman, but I managed to help her to her feet and walk her into the parlor where she collapsed on the sofa. Liddy put a pillow under her head and covered her with one of those knitted blankets with holes in them, that I learned later is called an afghan, that had been flung over the back of the sofa.

Liddy hurried from the room and came back in a moment with a glass of water. Mrs. Jenkins took it gratefully and drank a couple of swallows and handed it back.

"What happened?" Liddy asked.

"He hit me. That man hit me," Mrs. Jenkins said.

"What man?" Liddy asked.

"I don't know. I never saw him before. I heard someone knock at the door and when I answered it he pushed his way in and when I tried to stop him he hit me. The next thing I knew I was lying on the floor in the hallway. I had managed to sit up by the time you got here but that's all I know."

"Do you remember what he looked like, ma'am?" I asked.

"I hardly got a look at him," she said. "He wasn't as big as you and I think he had dark hair. He didn't say anything, he just hit me."

"Ma'am," I said, "if yer feelin' up to it you might look around and see if he took anything, see if anything's missin'."

I helped her to her feet and she looked around the room. "Doesn't seem to be anything missing here. Let me check the other rooms."

I went to help her but she shook me off. "I'm all right now," she said. "He didn't hurt me all that bad. I was shocked as much as anything. No man has ever hit me before. Mr. Jenkins, God rest his soul, never laid a hand on me in thirty years of marriage."

She went off to check the other rooms, and I turned to Liddy. "Maybe you'd better check your room," I suggested.

"Oh," she said. "I never thought . . ." The sentence trailed off as she hurried out of the room.

In a minute I heard her say, "Oh, no!" and I followed the sound of her voice down the hall to her bedroom. She was standing in the middle of her room, which had been torn apart.

"What do you suppose he was looking for?" I asked.

"I don't know. I don't have anything of value. Just a couple of pieces of jewelry my mother left me and they're here." She reached down to the floor and picked up a gold necklace and a ring with a very small diamond in it.

I noticed that her clothes were still neatly hanging in her closet.

"I don't think he finished looking," I said. "We must of scared him off. Look, the window is open."

I went over to it and looked out. The shrubbery under the window had been broken as if someone had stepped in it. But there was no sign of anyone and the ground was too hard for whoever it was to have left any discernible prints. And even if he'd left some, it wouldn't have meant anything to me. I've heard of some Western men who could track a snake across a flat rock, but that wasn't me. I'm pretty good with a gun or a knife or a rope but you want me to follow someone, he'd better be in seeing or hearing distance if you expect me to find him.

We trooped back to the parlor.

"You got any law here we can call on?" I asked Mrs. Jenkins.

"We have a sheriff and town marshal both, but I don't know what they can do about this. They're just old cowboys who got lawman jobs. They don't know much about tracking down criminals, 'specially when I can't say what the man looked like."

It only taken Liddy a few minutes to put her room in order and put together a bundle of her things. Mrs. Jenkins said she would be all right and promised to keep her doors and windows locked, so we told her goodbye and walked back to Ada Venn's cottage.

After promising to return in time for dinner I taken Old Dobbin to the livery stable where a lanky young man with bad teeth and equally bad breath took my 50 cents and promised to rub him down and give him a bait of oats. From there I walked down the street to the Texan Hotel and asked for a room. I drew my name laboriously on the register, taken my key from a young and pretty little woman behind the counter, and went up the stairs to my room where I deposited my saddlebags on the floor and myself on the bed.

CHAPTER 2

I HAD NO SOONER begun to doze off when there was a hard knock on my door.

"Go away," I called.

A voice came through the closed door. "Open up, Sackett. This is the law talkin'."

Dang, I said to myself. One thing about Ma, she'd been death on swearing, and whilst I backslid once in a while I'd always tried to keep from using curse words out of respect for her. So "dang" was usually about as much as I said unless I'd plumb run out of temper.

I got off of the bed, tromped over to the door, and opened it.

"Name ain't Sackett," I said to the stocky, red-faced man who was standing there.

He wore a badge on a beat-up old cowhide vest and two guns tied down low.

"I guess not," he said. "I seen your name on the register downstairs and thought maybe you was one of that family of gunfighters and was usin' an alias for some reason or other. Howsomever, I seen a couple of 'em in my time and you sure ain't one of 'em. Yer big enough but yer too ugly."

"You ain't no raving beauty yerownself," I said. "What can I do for ya?"

"Get out of town," he said.

I looked at him in surprise. "That ain't very neighborly," I said. "I just got here."

"You been here too long already," he said.

A sudden light dawned. "Crispen Giucy?" I asked.

"Yer smarter'n you look."

"He tell you he was beatin' up on a woman?"

"If that's true, tell her to press charges."

"You know she won't do that. She's scared half to death. Besides, it looks to me like Giucy has the law in this town in his hip pocket."

The marshal's face got redder still. "Mister, I'm paid to do a job and I do it. Right now my job is to see that you leave town."

"Marshal," I said, "I ain't never bucked the law, leastwise when it was honest I ain't. Ma, she raised me that way. I'll be leavin' in the mornin' if that suits you."

"That suits me," he said. "But if I find you moseyin' around town tonight lookin' for trouble I'll throw you in jail without thinkin' twice and throw the key away."

He turned and stomped down the hall to the stairs. I watched him go, then on an impulse I followed him down and went over to the pretty little woman at the counter. The big Regulator wall clock said it was just turning six o'clock, which meant I had enough time.

"Ma'am," I said, "I need a bath quick. Can I get one?"

"That'll be a quarter," she said.

I followed her directions down a hallway to a room with a tub and mirror and some hooks on the wall. In a minute an old Negro man came in carrying buckets of hot water. After three trips he had the tub filled and in a minute he was back with soap and a big towel.

He set them down but showed no signs of leaving until I took the hint and handed him another quarter. Ma used to say that cleanliness is next to godliness, but she neglected to add that sometimes it can be more expensive.

I had another shirt, worn, but clean, in my saddlebags, along

18

with a change of underwear and socks that I'd been saving for an occasion like this. Up there in the Sierras when I was growing up I didn't wear socks because I didn't have any to wear but after I went out on my own I'd taken to wearing them. Everybody, I guess, needs some sort of luxury, and socks were mine.

By the time I'd bathed and shaved and dressed I was feeling pretty much like a new man, so I dumped my gear back in my room, strapped on my hideaway knife that I wore in a sheath strapped to the inside of my right leg just above my ankle, buckled on my gun belt, and took off for Ada Venn's cottage.

It was still light when I got there and I was just unlatching the gate when that spotted mongrel came off the porch with a rush, barking and growling, with his hackles raised. I quick shut the gate and got my hand off of it before the mutt could nip it.

Ada Venn came to the door of the cottage and hollered, "Henry, be quiet and leave him alone."

Henry gave a last growl and trotted back to the porch. Ada called to me to come in and I did so warily, but Henry had had his say and now he was lying down again on a corner of the porch.

Ada greeted me at the door. "Come in," she said, taking my hat. "My, don't you look nice. I'm so glad you could come."

"Henry?" I said.

"When I was a little girl I always had a hankering for a dog," she explained. "So when I finally got one I named him Henry, thinking I would call him Hank, but it turned out that I liked Henry better."

"I see," I said, polite-like, not really seeing at all.

She saw that I didn't see and said, "It's kind of a pun. You know, a play on words."

"I'm sorry, ma'am," I said. "You got me wadin' in deep water here. Henry's fine by me, just so long as he don't bite."

"I'm sorry, too," she said. "I don't mean to talk over your head."

As usual, my ignorance had embarrassed me, but if she noticed she paid no attention. Instead, she took me by the arm and walked me into the parlor where she sat on the sofa and pulled me down beside her.

"I'm so glad you could come," she repeated, staring at me earnestly. "It's nice to have a man in the house once in a while. Besides, Liddy and I are both terribly grateful to you. I don't know what we'd have done today without you."

"That's right," Liddy said from the doorway. "I don't know what we'd have done either."

Her face fell and her shoulders sagged a mite. "And I don't know what we'll do when you're gone."

"Speakin' of goin'," I said, "the marshal come around almost as soon as I got to the hotel and tried to run me out of town. Threatened to throw me in jail. I told him I'd be leavin' in the mornin'. He as much as admitted that Giucy give him his orders."

"I'm not surprised," Ada said bitterly. "Marshal Coleman is ordinarily a very nice man and competent as well. But Mr. Giucy got him his job after he lost his ranch to the bank. So he does just about what Mr. Giucy tells him to do."

"Figures," I said. "What about the sheriff? He in Giucy's pocket, too?"

Liddy spoke up. "Sheriff Fothergill? He couldn't be. He and Father rode together in the Rangers. He's as honest as the day is long. Not only that, he preaches on Sundays at a little church at Coyote Junction, about 10 miles south of here. He's not ordained; he's what they call a lay minister. He's talked to me about going to seminary when his children are grown and becoming ordained. So you see, he couldn't be in anybody's—what did you say? Pocket? He couldn't be in anybody's pocket. Unless maybe the Lord's."

"As long as he ain't in Giucy's," I said.

"It's an interesting combination," Ada said with a smile. "If he can't save you he can always arrest you. And once he's got you in a cell he can preach at you all day long."

Ada ignored a disapproving look from Liddy and stood up. "It's time for supper," she said.

Liddy and I followed her into a tiny dining room where she had a table set for three with a real cloth tablecloth that turned out to be linen and tableware that turned out to be sterling silver.

During dinner Ada explained that she had inherited the sterling from her mother and, a bit ruefully, that the tablecloth had been in her hope chest until the day she had faced reality and given up hope. Looking at her, that was hard for me to understand. She was a handsome woman, a warm woman, and seemed to be every bit a lady. Some women, I guess, just weren't meant to be married. And in her case I thought that was too bad. It seemed to me she'd make some man a mighty fine wife.

I'm not much on manners, having come out of the California mountains the way I had, and Ma always being too tired from panning for gold all day long to pay much attention to that sort of thing. But I knew enough to seat the ladies before I sat down. And I watched the two of them to see how they handled their eating tools.

Ada did most of the talking, for the most part, I thought, because she could see I was a mite uncomfortable and was trying to put me at ease. She served a good meal, too, none of those dainty portions some people serve only because they're putting on airs.

We had roast beef and mashed potatoes and gravy and peas, which I found a little hard to eat because they kept rolling around on my plate. For dessert she brought out slices of chocolate cake which, she explained, she'd bought at a little cafe in town where the cook prided himself on his pastries.

After we ate, her and Liddy sat there drinking tea but she'd made a pot of coffee for me. Liddy had been pretty quiet during the meal, and now Ada asked her what her plans were.

"I don't know," she said. "I'm afraid to go back to Mrs. Jenkins' house because of that man and I'm afraid to go to school tomorrow because of Mr. Giucy. I just don't know."

"That feller must have wanted somethin'," I said. "It don't seem logical that he'd bust in there and tear things apart unless he wanted somethin'. I think we scared him off before he could find what he was after. He hadn't got to yer closet yet. Would there be somethin' in there?"

"Just my clothes," she said, "and the little bundle of papers and things that belonged to Father that Miss Rankin sent from the ranch. I've never gotten around to looking through them, but how could there possibly be anything there that anyone would want?"

"You'll never know unless you look," Ada murmured.

I was beginning to get the impression that Ada was maybe a little impatient with Liddy, probably because she was older and more sophisticated. But, if Liddy had sensed her feeling, she paid no attention to it.

Instead she said, "You're right. I brought them with me so why don't I get them now?" and hurried from the room.

Ada looked at me. "Amazing, isn't it? She's had those papers all this time and never looked at them. I couldn't do that. I'd be too curious."

I didn't know what to say. I'd been carrying that diary of Ma's around with me for almost a year and hadn't looked at it. My problem wasn't a lack of interest, though; it was because I couldn't read. One reason I'd come to Abilene to meet Liddy Doyle was to see if maybe she was the person who could teach me. From my way of thinking it couldn't be just anybody and certainly not nobody I was going to live around or be friends with. Being ignorant like that was embarrassing to me and I didn't want people I cared about knowing it and trying to help me.

Esmeralda Rankin had found out about it back at the R Bar R and had offered to read the diary for me, and when I turned her down had offered to teach me to read. But I was in love with her and I didn't think it right that a man should have to turn to his woman to teach him things he ought to know anyway. I know a lot of folks will think that was kind of a stupid attitude—and maybe it was—but that's how I felt and I couldn't help it.

I must have looked kind of funny because Ada asked, "Don't you agree?"

Just then Liddy came back into the room carrying a small bundle that was wrapped in brown paper and tied with string. She carefully untied the string and smoothed the brown paper out on the table. Esmeralda had sandwiched the bundle between two pieces of cardboard to keep it from wrinkling and tearing. Now, Liddy set the top piece aside and picked up the first item. It was a tally book filled with notes in an awkward left-handed writing. Billy Bob Doyle had been right-handed and when he'd lost his right arm he'd had to learn to write left-handed.

Liddy scanned it quickly but after a minute or two set it down.

"There isn't anything there," she said. "Just notes about cattle and range conditions on the R Bar R ranch."

Next there was an old tintype photograph of a young and pretty woman. Liddy looked at it gravely and handed it to me. "My mother," she said.

"Pretty lady," I said. "You look a lot like her."

All that remained were half a dozen envelopes. Three were letters from Liddy that he'd kept. The fourth was a letter from a lawyer in Denver that read:

"Our client, Mr. Oscar Taime, has instructed us to notify you that in return for saving him from drowning on May 9, 1879, he has deeded a 50 percent share of his silver mine, The Wait and See, to you, Mr. William Robert Doyle, effective this day, June 10, 1881. The Wait and See is located at Bonanza, Colo. A deed for your 50 percent share of said The Wait and See mine is being held in our offices and may be claimed by you at any time upon presentation of proper identification. Sincerely, Kooby Rarbil, atty. at law."

The fifth envelope contained a short letter from Oscar Taime. It had no date but it was obviously written at about the same time Rarbil had written his letter. Liddy read:

"Dere Billy Bob: I ain't never forgot that you saved my life. Mebbe now I kin repay you. I have found a vane of silver ore and have staked a claim. I found me a lawyer to fix up a legal deed giving you haf of it. Cum and join me. Mebbe we'll both be rich.

Yer frend, Oscar."

The last letter had never been opened. Esmeralda Rankin had written on it: "Dear Miss Doyle: This letter arrived after your father's death. E.R."

The letter was from the law firm of Rarbil, Tomes & Emulov in Denver. Clearly, over the years Mr. Rarbil had expanded and prospered. Liddy went to the kitchen and returned with a knife and carefully slit open the letter.

It, too, was signed by Kooby Rarbil. It was a long letter saying that Oscar Taime had died, leaving no will, and that a year-long search had finally unearthed Taime's only living relative, a distant cousin in Abilene, Tex., named Crispen Giucy. Mr. Giucy, the letter went on, had been notified that he had inherited half ownership in "The Wait and See" mine, the value of which currently was assessed at in excess of a million dollars.

"He has also been notified that you, William Robert Doyle, are a half owner of the mine with all profits being shared equally and management decisions to be made jointly." Finally, the letter said, there was $50,000 in the Bonanza Bank in the name of William Robert Doyle and that he should notify the bank of his current address and how he wanted the money handled. The money, the letter explained, was Billy Bob's share of the net profits from the mine.

"Fifty thousand dollars," Liddy said. "That's a lot of money. Father wrote to me once about the mine but he said he was sure he'd never get any money out of it. But he was wrong, wasn't he? I'm so sorry he didn't live to get the money. He deserved a chance to take life easy."

"While you're figuring out what you're going to do I'll go make some more tea," Ada said. "Would you like another cup of coffee, Del?"

"Yes'm," I said. "That is surely good coffee."

While Ada was gone I said to Liddy, "Seems to me you've solved one mystery, anyway."

"You mean we know why Mr. Giucy wants to marry me?"

"It's a rich mine. Seems to me he ain't willin' to settle for half a loaf."

"Oh, dear," she said. "I wonder what I ought to do."

Ada Venn, coming in with the tea and coffee, heard her. "Why not sleep on it?" she said. "This whole thing is such a big surprise we're probably not any of us thinking clearly."

She turned to me. "Mr. Tackett—Del—I have a big favor to ask of you. Now that we think we know what Mr. Giucy is after I'm a little worried about Liddy and me being alone tonight. Could you possibly stay over?"

She taken me by surprise. "I . . . I don't know, Ada. Don't seem proper I should spend the night with two unmarried women."

She laughed. "There's safety and propriety in numbers, Del. Please, won't you stay? I know we'll be perfectly safe with you and Henry here but without you somebody could kill Henry very easily, either with a gun or with poison, and then we'd be helpless."

"Well," I said reluctantly, "I understand how ya feel. I guess in yer situation I'd be a little uneasy, too. I'll stay."

"It's just for tonight," she said. "Tomorrow we'll work things out."

I finished my coffee and she and Liddy drank the rest of their tea and I stood up and said, "Been a long day. If you'll show me my room . . ."

"All of a sudden I'm quite sleepy, too," Liddy said.

"You can share my bedroom, Liddy," Ada told her. "I'll show you to your room, Del."

It was a small room, but it had a big bed in it that turned out to be real comfortable. In about five minutes I was stripped down to my long johns and lying under the covers. Being pure of heart and with a clear conscience I dropped off almost as quick as my head hit the pillow.

I don't know how long I'd been sleeping when something— likely a creaking floorboard—awoke me.

I sat up, mentally cussing myself for leaving my gun belt hanging on a chair across the room. I had to have been tired to do anything that dumb.

A woman's voice murmured, "It's all right, Del. It's Ada." She quickly moved over and sat on the edge of the bed.

"What is it?" I asked. "What's wrong?"

"Nothing," she said, caressing my arm. "I couldn't sleep and I'm lonely and I know you're lonely too."

I panicked. "Ma'am, I'm sorry, but this ain't right."

"Of course it's right," she said. "The way I feel now I need you desperately and I'd be very surprised if you didn't need me just as badly."

"But . . ." I said.

"But nothing. Everything is just fine. I put something in Liddy's tea and she'll sleep the night through.

"Del, I'm lonely and I need someone to hold me and love me. You needn't worry. I'm no virgin."

I felt myself turning red in the dark. No woman had ever talked like that to me before.

But before I could say anything Ada moved quickly and I caught a glimpse of bare flesh as she pulled her nightgown over her head. Before I knew it she was under the covers and had pulled me down to her, her lips seeking mine and her body pressing hard against me.

There are times and places and situations that, when they all come together at once, there's nothing much a body can do but just accept what's happening. This was one of those times.

CHAPTER 3

As USUAL I WOKE at the first blush of dawn and, as usual, I was all alone. For a brief moment I thought I might have been dreaming but then I knew I wasn't. Even my most vivid dreams have never been that real.

I got out of bed and dressed as quietly as possible, meaning to sneak out of the house before either of the women was up. But I hadn't gotten close to the front door before Ada's voice from the kitchen stopped me.

"Good morning, Del," she said cheerily. "The coffee is ready."

Not having much choice I turned and went into the kitchen. She had a fire going in the cookstove and the smell of coffee was in the air. She looked especially pretty, her hair was down instead of up in a bun the way it had been yesterday, and she didn't look hardly any older than Liddy.

"Mornin', Ada," I said, "about last night . . ."

She crossed the room to me and put a finger to my lips. "Don't say anything, Del. It was wonderful for me, but as far as you and I are concerned it never happened. Even though I will never forget it."

She reached up with both hands and pulled my head down and kissed me lightly on the lips. "I'll pour your coffee," she said.

I sat down at the kitchen table and watched her as she went about preparing breakfast. This here was quite a woman, maybe not the woman for me, but still, quite a woman.

She put some eggs and bacon and fried potatoes down in front of me and sat drinking coffee while I ate. She wasn't eating, she said, because she was never hungry in the morning, "even though this is one of those mornings when I ought to be hungry."

I didn't say anything, just looked down at my plate and kept on eating. Finally I finished and looked up.

"Thought mebbe me and Liddy might drop around and see Sheriff Fothergill this mornin', if, like you say, he's an honest man. Mebbe he can make sure you ladies are safe until Liddy can take care of her business with them lawyers."

"I think Liddy had better get to Bonanza right away, before Crispen Giucy figures out a way to get his hands on her money and her half of the mine," Ada said.

"Yer probably right," I said. "But I still need to see the sheriff."

"What do you need to see Sheriff Fothergill for?" Liddy asked coming into the room.

She was a beauty. Her red hair was brushed until it shone like copper wire and her green eyes were bright. She didn't wait for an answer.

"That's a comfortable bed you have, Ada. I slept like a log. I thought I was going to toss and turn all night worrying about the mine and the money and Crispen Giucy. But I went right off to sleep.

"What are we going to do about the mine and the money and Crispen Giucy? And why do you need to see the sheriff, Del?"

"Thought mebbe if I explained the situation to him he could keep an eye on the two of you. I've done what I come here to do and it's time I was moseyin' along."

Their faces fell. "You can't go now," Liddy said. "We need you. I was hoping you would go to Bonanza with me, if that's what we think I should do. I could pay you after I get my money."

"That's a long trip," I said. "First thing you ought to do is send a wire to that Rarbil feller, explainin' the situation and askin' for his advice. From his letter it sounded like he might be honest, even though Ma used to say, 'Never trust a lawyer.' "

"What did your mother know about lawyers?" Ada asked curiously.

"Danged if I know. Wasn't none of them hangin' around Lodestone when I was growin' up. But Ma come from the East and she might of known one or two of 'em there."

"If I wire Mr. Rarbil and he says to go to Bonanza will you go there with me?" Liddy pleaded.

"I think you should," Ada said. "That's a long way for a woman to travel alone."

"Besides," she added, looking at me knowingly, "on a long trip like that maybe Liddy could be of some help to you."

Now what did she mean by that, I wondered. Then it came to me. Lying there in that big bed last night with Ada snuggled next to me the two of us had done some talking. She told me how the man she was going to marry had contracted tuberculosis and had gone West to the dry country around Phoenix for his health and had promised to send for her when he was better. Six months later a letter had come saying he had died. Before he left, she said, they'd thrown caution to the winds, knowing that one day they would be married, and had spent a night together. "The most wonderful night of my life," she said, "until tonight."

Well, I just naturally started telling her about myself and at some point I'd mentioned that I couldn't hardly read or write and I'd hoped that when I found Liddy she might be able to teach me.

"If you stay in Abilene one or both of us will be glad to teach you," she said. "I . . . we owe you a lot. More than you'll ever know."

That had been last night. I was glad Liddy didn't know what Ada was referring to.

Ada looked at an old mantlepiece clock sitting over the fireplace and said it was time for her to go open the schoolhouse. After school, she said, she would have to find the mayor and see what could be done about recruiting a second teacher since it was clear that Liddy would not be available to teach, at least for two or three months—never if everything went right in Bonanza.

I offered to walk her to school but she said she would put a leash on Henry and take him to school with her. "Nobody is going to bother me in the daylight with Henry along," she said.

Before she left she said, "I imagine that it will be two or three days before you and Liddy can leave. If that's the case, why don't you plan to stay here? It doesn't cost as much and the food is better."

I thought quick about getting married, about having children, about making an honest woman out of Ada, about Esme. "I think I'd best be stayin' at the hotel," I said.

"Well, think about it anyway," she urged, looking at me with soft eyes. She snapped a leash on Henry and the two of them headed · off to the school.

When she'd gone Liddy said, "Was Ada acting a little odd this morning or was it my imagination?"

"Hard to say," I said. "I don't usually spend my mornin's here."

Liddy fetched a piece of paper and sat down to write a telegram to Kooby Rarbil. When she'd finished she handed it to me.

"Is that all right?" she asked.

I handed it back to her. "You read it to me. I ain't so good at readin' handwritin'."

She looked at me kind of funny. "I printed it," she said, "so the man at the train station wouldn't have any trouble reading it."

"I don't read printin' so well, either," I said grudgingly.

"You're teasing," she said, smiling.

"I can't read, dang it," I shouted. "I just can't read. Now are ya happy?"

I turned and started for the door, mad at myself and feeling like a fool.

She followed me and caught me by the sleeve. "Don't go, Del.

I'm sorry. I didn't mean to embarrass you. I didn't mean to make you angry."

I stopped and faced her. "I ain't mad at you. I'm mad at myself. I feel like a dang fool. Here I am a growed man and I can't hardly read or write or even speak decent."

"Is that what Ada meant when she said I might be of some help to you on a long trip?"

I lied then. "Might be. I ain't exactly sure what she meant. Maybe she noticed I wasn't readin' nothin' last night."

"Let me read you what I wrote," she said.

Dear Mr. Rarbil. Several months ago you wrote to my father, William Robert Doyle, informing him of the death of his partner, Oscar Taime, and notifying him that $50,000 has been deposited in the bank in Bonanza, Colo. in his name. My father was killed before your letter arrived and I have just received it. As his heir I wish to claim the money as well as his share of The Wait and See mine.

Please wire me instructions. (signed) Elizabeth Doyle.

"Sounds fine to me," I said.

We left the house and walked on into town, detouring by the stable first to make sure that Old Dobbin was being well taken care of. From there it was just a few minutes' walk to the sheriff's office. It turned out that the town marshal, Wick Coleman, shared an office with Sheriff Fothergill. Both of them were in.

Coleman looked up when we entered. "Mornin', Miss Elizabeth," he said. Then he saw me. "Thought I told you to get out of town," he growled.

"I got business with the sheriff here, so back off, Marshal," I said.

"Don't tell me to back off," he said, coming to his feet. "I told you last night, you got a choice. Get out of town or go to jail."

Sheriff Fothergill looked up from his paperwork. "Trouble?" he asked mildly.

"Nothin' that I can't handle," Coleman said

"Sheriff Fothergill," I said, "I'm Del Tackett. Will you tell this here loudmouth to shut up so's you and me can talk?"

"By God, you can't call me a loudmouth," Coleman snarled, going into a crouch like he wanted to reach for his guns.

"Wick," Fothergill said, "there's a lady present. Why don't you let Mr. Sackett here state his business? Then, if there's a reason for him to leave town, I'm sure he'll be glad to go."

Coleman sank back in his chair. "He's outta here as soon as he finishes his business. Besides, he ain't no Sackett. Name is Tackett."

"That's right, Sheriff," I said. "Name is Tackett. I ain't no gunfighter. Just a wanderin' cowpoke."

"Giucy says you was purty quick to draw on him yesterday," Coleman said.

"Don't like to see a man abusin' a lady," I said. "Besides, if I'd of hit him with my fist he might of hit me back and we might of tore up the schoolroom. And I didn't want that, me bein' a respecter of education and all. The way it was there wasn't no trouble."

Fothergill whistled. "You drew a gun on Crispen Giucy. No wonder he wants you out of town. I'd suggest you go, Tackett. Even a Sackett wouldn't be smart to hang around here after crossing Giucy."

"Ain't nobody ever accused me of bein' smart, Sheriff," I said. "But I'm smart enough not to want to talk here in front of Giucy's hired hand. Mebbe you and me and Miss Liddy could go get a cup of coffee."

"Sounds good to me," Fothergill said, rising and offering Liddy his arm. Coleman gave me a dirty look, but I paid him no mind and followed Liddy and Fothergill out the door. There was a restaurant up the street a couple of doors and we went in and found a table in a corner.

The waitress, a slight girl who looked about sixteen, brought three cups of coffee. It was hot and black and tasted good.

Fothergill wasn't much to look at until you saw his eyes which were blue and gazed right through you. He was average height, about five foot nine, and slight of build. His sandy hair was receding. His face was tanned and weather-beaten with deep crows-feet at the corners of rather narrow eyes. I took him to be around forty. He wore one gun which he had tucked almost casually behind his belt. He didn't look like a gunslinger but he had an air of calm confidence about him that told me he was one man I didn't want to tangle with.

He wore black jeans and a shirt that was open at the collar. And I noticed with surprise that around his neck he wore a gold chain to which was attached a small golden cross. Then I remembered what Liddy had told me last night: This was a devout Christian man who enforced the law six days a week and preached on Sundays. Years later, when I knew him better, he told me he thought there were three essentials when it came to building a civilization on the frontier: Education, religion, and law enforcement.

"And there's no room for either education or religion in a lawless land," he said. "So while I preach on Sundays to save man's immortal soul, I enforce the law the rest of the time so that we can educate our children and build our land."

But today he wasn't philosophizing and while he was wearing a cross on a chain around his neck he wasn't wearing his religion on his sleeve.

"Now," he said, "before you tell me what's on your mind, let me tell you how things are run here. Wick Coleman enforces the law in town and I don't butt in unless I'm asked or unless I run into someone actually committing a crime. My territory is the county— the range and the little unincorporated towns and crossroads.

"I don't have anything to do with the town council, including

Crispen Giucy, and I don't take orders from them. Just like them, I'm elected. Coleman, on the other hand, is appointed by them and he happens to be Giucy's man. It doesn't mean he's a bad man. He pretty generally does a good job here but he looks the other way as far as Giucy is concerned.

"Now, what's on your mind?"

"Mebbe I better start from the beginnin'," I said.

So I told him how I'd come to town yesterday, omitting that one reason was that I was hoping I could get Liddy to teach me to read, and how at the school I'd found Crispen Giucy laying hands on Ada Venn and threatening her and how I'd run him out of the school. I told him how Liddy had been afraid to go to school because Giucy had threatened to hurt her if she didn't marry him and how, when we went to Mrs. Jenkins', we arrived after someone had knocked her down and had ransacked Liddy's room.

"We think he was lookin' for a bundle of Liddy's pa's stuff that was sent to her after he was killed," I said.

Liddy took over from there. "I hadn't looked at it because I didn't think there was anything there," she said and went on to explain what we'd found.

"I don't think Crispen Giucy loves me," she said bitterly. "He wanted to marry me just to get my share of the mine and when I wouldn't marry him he decided to resort to violence."

"You report any of this to Coleman?" Fothergill asked.

"Didn't seem to make much sense, him bein', like you yourself say, in Giucy's pocket," I said.

Fothergill nodded thoughtfully. "Coleman say why he wanted you out of town?"

"Didn't have to. I knowed."

"It doesn't seem right," the sheriff said. "How long were you figuring on staying around?"

"Hadn't made up my mind when I come here," I said. "But now, one way or another I'm gonna stay until Miss Liddy here decides what she's gonna do. After that, I don't know. I ain't never been much for lettin' someone try to run me off."

Fothergill beckoned the skinny little waitress over to refill our cups. "I have an idea," he said. "Have you ever been a lawman?"

"I was a actin' town marshal once for a couple of months while the real marshal was recoverin' from a bullet wound but that's all. It wasn't much of a town and there wasn't much action during the time I had the job."

"It's enough," he said. "Come on back to the office with me. I'm going to swear you in as a deputy sheriff. That ought to take care of things for as long as you expect to be around. It won't pay anything and I may ask you to do a little work just to make it legitimate. Sunday might be a good day to pitch in."

"Thought maybe I could help you preach on Sundays," I said.

He smiled. "So you know what else I do. Sorry, but I don't think you'd be comfortable in church. If you'll enforce the law on Sundays you'll be doing the Lord's work that way."

"I ain't sure the Lord would have me," I said, tossing a quarter on the table and getting to my feet.

The three of us traipsed back to the sheriff's office. Marshal Coleman had gone out somewhere so there was just the three of us as Fothergill dug a deputy's badge out of his desk drawer and pinned it on the beat-up old denim vest I was wearing.

"Hold up your right hand," he directed. "You swear to uphold and enforce the laws of the United States and Texas and this county and to make sure other folks do the same?"

"I do," I said.

"You're now a deputy sheriff with all rights and duties pertaining thereto," he said with a smile. "That ought to help for as long as you're in town. And I hope that isn't too long.

"Just a couple more things, then I have to go take care of a matter over at Bountyville. Been a shooting over there.

"First, while I'm gone, if there's trouble in county territory I expect you to handle it. If it's here in town leave it to Coleman unless he asks for help which I don't think he will.

"Second, I'm assigning you to guard Miss Doyle and Miss Venn. They are your personal responsibility. And, third, try to stay out of trouble."

"Sheriff," I said, "I can handle everything exceptin' the stay out of trouble part. I can't promise that. I ain't gonna look for it. Never do. But when it comes lookin' for me it always seems to find me and I just naturally have a hard time backin' away from it."

"Do your best," he said.

CHAPTER 4

AFTER THANKING the sheriff for his help, Liddy and I headed down the street to the train station. I noticed some folks on the street looking funny-like at her.

Finally she turned to me and said, "They wonder why I'm not at school. What shall I say if someone asks?"

"Tell 'em the truth," I said. "Some family business come up unexpected-like and you got to take care of it."

"I'm so glad Ada is a good teacher," she said. "She can handle both classrooms for a few days, I know. And she is such a dear friend. I don't know what I'd do without her. Or you."

"You'd figure somethin'," I said, holding open the door of the station so she could enter first.

The station master, who doubled as the telegrapher and ticket seller and janitor, looked at us from behind the counter. On our side of it, slouched in a chair which was tilted back against the wall, was Marshal Wick Coleman, cleaning his fingernails with the small blade of a Barlow folding knife. When he saw me he leaned forward bringing the front legs of his chair down on the floor with a crash. In the same movement he came lunging to his feet.

"How many times I got to tell you to get out of town?" he rasped.

Then he saw the badge on my vest and did a double take. "Where the hell did you get that badge?" he demanded.

I grinned at him. "I'm Fothergill's new deputy, Marshal. He

done swore me in a little while ago. Miss Liddy here witnessed it. I'm here to help enforce the law."

"In a pig's eye," he snarled. "That damn badge don't mean a thing here in town. I done told you to get out of town for the last time. Now I'm takin' you in."

"I got business here, Marshal," I said. "And I aim to take care of it."

He took a step toward me. "Not now you ain't. Yer comin' with me."

He made a mistake then. He reached out to grab my right arm leaving his jaw exposed. I saw it and just naturally threw a left hook at it with most of my weight behind the punch. He stumbled backwards for a couple of steps then went down on his right arm and shoulder with his head banging against the board wall of the station. He struggled for a bit to get up, but then sank back, too dazed and shaken to make it.

"Ask the man to send yer wire, Liddy," I said without taking my eyes off the marshal.

I heard the station master say, "Now, see here. I won't have any violence in my station."

"Send the lady's wire," I said, without looking around.

"There's other business ahead of her. I can't do it now," he said.

I walked over to where Coleman was just beginning to sit up and reached down and taken both his guns which I slid across the room, making it difficult for him, was he to get to feeling brave.

"Stay there and keep quiet," I said to him. Then I went over to the counter where the station master stood. He was average size, average build, average looks with a hook nose and a weak chin. He wore a green eyeshade. I reached over and taken him by the front of his shirt.

"Send the lady's wire," I said, pulling him halfway over the counter.

"Y-y-yes sir," he said.

Liddy silently handed him what she'd written and he took it over to the little Morse Code instrument on his desk and began punching the key.

When he'd finished I said, "Give the lady back her writin'."

He picked it up and handed it back to her.

"I'm going to report this to the proper authorities," he sputtered. "You can't come into my station and bully people and push them around."

"Tell you what, Mister," I said, taking out my gun. "You report to anyone you want, but if the lady don't hear back from that wire in two days I got me an authority right here that you'll answer to and I don't think you'll like it. Furthermore, that wire ain't nobody's business but the lady's and don't you ferget it."

He turned pale, started to say something, but thought better of it. I turned to Wick Coleman who was sitting up glaring at me.

"Marshal," I said, "you might not believe this, but I got a lot of respect for the law. But that don't mean that you or anyone else with a tin badge on is goin' to push me around. Now I don't intend to stay in this town very long. But as long as I'm here and not causin' anyone any trouble you walk wide of me. Hear?

"And that goes for Crispen Giucy, too.

"Come on, Liddy, I'll walk you home."

She didn't say anything as we left the station and when I glanced at her she was looking straight ahead with a distant expression on her face.

"What ya thinkin' about?" I asked.

"Nothing," she said. "Nothing. Yes, I am. I'm thinking that you're a man who loves violence. You're a man who would rather hit somebody or even shoot him rather than talk to him like a rational human being."

Well, that kind of taken me aback for a minute.

Finally, I said, "Liddy, this here is a rough country and there ain't much here in the way of civilization. It's gettin' civilized, but

we ain't there yet. You take them two back there at the station.
Wick Coleman was lookin' for trouble. I ain't done nothin' to get
arrested for, but Coleman, he takes orders from Crispen Giucy,
and Giucy wants me outta here. If I hadn't hit him Coleman would
have me behind bars right now, and let me tell you jail ain't no fun
place to be. I been there once or twice and I know.

"Now you take that station master. He was cozyin' up to Coleman and probably is takin' money from Giucy. You can bet he's
goin' to tell him about yer wire. And about the answer. But I put
the fear of God in him and he dang well won't try to stall you when
you go to get it."

"I think you're exaggerating," she said. "We are civilized here.
We have a city council and a mayor and a school and everybody
says Marshal Coleman does a good job. And you certainly had no
reason to manhandle that little man at the station."

"Well, I guess that takes care of that," I said. "I'll see you to your
place or Ada's, whichever you want, then I'll be movin' along."

"I'll be going to Mrs. Jenkins' house," she said stiffly. "After
that I'll be fine. I want to thank you for coming and for your help
yesterday."

I didn't answer and we walked in silence to Mrs. Jenkins' house.
I left her at the gate, watched her halfway up the walk, and turned
and strode away, mad. I'd gone about a hundred feet when I heard
her scream. I ain't no sprinter but I might have set a record for
getting there. I leaped the fence, twisted my ankle and nearly went
down, righted myself, went up the steps in one bound, and burst
through the front door.

Liddy Doyle was standing in the parlor, holding one hand to her
face and looking down on Mrs. Jenkins who was lying on her back
on the parlor rug. She was dead. Her dress was torn, her face was
discolored, and her wide open eyes were bulging. She'd been
strangled.

So much for civilization, I thought.

Liddy turned to me, her face dead white, her eyes staring. "Oh, it's you," she said. "Thank God you came back."

I looked around the room. It had been torn apart pretty good.

"Wait here a minute," I said. "I want to take a look around."

I went into Liddy's bedroom first. It, too, had been torn apart and searched thoroughly. So, I found as I went from room to room, had the rest of the house—Mrs. Jenkins' bedroom, the kitchen, the dining room. They looked like a tornado had hit them. Whoever had killed Mrs. Jenkins, and I figured it was the same man who'd broken in yesterday, was looking for something, and clearly hadn't found it.

A sudden thought hit me. If whoever it was hadn't found what he was looking for here, where would he look next? I didn't have to ask twice. I already had the answer. Ada Venn's house.

For just a second I thought about sending Liddy for the sheriff while I went to Ada's but then I remembered he'd left town. Besides, I was now scared for her life, scared to leave her alone. Anyone who'd kill an old lady like Mrs. Jenkins wouldn't hesitate to kill anyone else who got in his way.

I took her arm. "Come on," I ordered, "we're goin' to Ada's place. Ain't nothin' we can do here now."

She started to resist. "But what about Mrs. Jenkins? Shouldn't we get the marshal or Sheriff Fothergill?"

"No time," I said, pulling her along. "We got to get to Ada's. Whoever was here didn't find what he wanted, which was probably the deed to the mine and the letter from that lawyer feller. My guess is the next place he'll look is Ada's. Let's go. And pray we ain't too late."

"Henry is there," she said. "He's a good watchdog."

I didn't even pause. "Ada taken Henry to school with her," I reminded.

When we got there Ada's front door was wide open. I swore silently to myself so neither Ma nor Liddy would hear. Out loud I said, "Dang."

And then I said to Liddy, "You stay here."

I drew my gun and went up the steps. In the parlor there was no sign that anyone had been there but I heard a slight noise in the back of the house, one of the bedrooms, but I didn't know which one. I tiptoed down the hall to the bedroom I'd slept in last night. I stood to one side and shoved the door open. The room was empty and hadn't been touched, but I'd pushed the door too hard and it banged against the wall with a thud.

That brought more noise from Ada's bedroom and I whirled, pushed that door open, and leaped inside. There was no one there but an open window and a fluttering curtain showed me where the intruder had gone. I ran to the window and looked out. No one in sight. Just then I heard Liddy cry, "Del," and then there was a shot.

I tore out of the room, down the short hall, through the parlor, and to the front door. Liddy was sitting on the top step, her face white, cradling her left arm which was oozing blood through her long-sleeved blouse. Fifty yards down the road a tall, hatless man with dark hair and wearing a dark shirt was disappearing in the distance. There wasn't any way I was going to catch him and it would take a lucky shot to hit him, but I taken one anyway and much to my surprise he kind of stumbled, then righted himself and kept on running.

I holstered my gun and turned to Liddy. "I don't think it's too bad," she said. "I think he just grazed me."

Then she fainted.

I leaned over her and took her hand away from her arm and pulled back her sleeve. She was almost right. The bullet had done more than graze her; it had cut a deep furrow in her arm but it had missed the bone. I picked her up and carried her into Ada's bedroom and laid her on the bed. In the kitchen I found a clean flour sack which I tore in strips and wrapped around her arm for a temporary bandage.

By this time she was coming to. She looked at me blankly for a moment, then all of a sudden she seemed to recollect what had happened. I lifted her head up and gave her a couple of swallows of water from a glass I'd brought from the kitchen. The color began coming back in her cheeks and she struggled to sit up, but I pushed her back down.

"Lie quiet," I said, "whilst I figure out what to do."

She lay back. "I fainted, didn't I?" she said. "I'm so embarrassed."

"Don't be," I said. "It takes a while to get used to gettin' shot at and hit."

She looked at me with big eyes. "I'm ashamed of myself for the way I acted a little while ago. I should have been grateful for your help and instead I berated you. Would you accept my apologies?"

"I don't blame you for gettin' upset," I said. "I know I was a mite rough back there, but there's some folks just don't understand nothin' else. They take bein' nice as a sign of weakness.

"I don't think that feller found what he was lookin' for. Where'd you put that package of stuff we looked at last night?"

"Ada took it. She said she would put it in a safe place. She didn't tell me where."

"Dang," I said. "I don't want to tear this place up lookin' for it. But we got to have it. You got to have it, that is."

Just then there was a loud rapping at the front door and a woman's voice called, "Miss Venn. Ada Venn."

"Dang," I said. "I guess I better go see what's happenin'."

A matronly looking woman in her thirties was standing at the open door.

"Who are you?" she asked.

"A friend of Miss Venn's," I answered. "I think you'll find her at school."

"That's just the trouble," she said. "She's supposed to be at school and she isn't. When she and Miss Doyle didn't show up this morning the children eventually went home. Several of the mothers came to me—I'm Mrs. Goshorn and I'm a member of the school board—and I thought I had better come see what is the matter. I went to Mrs. Jenkins' house to look for Miss Doyle but there was no one home."

Liddy Doyle's voice beside me said in surprise, "Mrs. Goshorn. What's wrong?"

"That's what I want to know. Why aren't you at school? And where is Miss Venn?" Mrs. Goshorn demanded.

"Isn't she at school?" Liddy asked.

"I would not be here if she were," Mrs. Goshorn said. Then she noticed Liddy's arm. "Oh, you're hurt."

"Ma'am," I said, "I think you better come in and sit down. There's some things going on here that don't make much sense. And some of it ain't very nice."

I stepped aside and Mrs. Goshorn came into the parlor and took a seat on the sofa.

"There ain't no easy way to tell you this," I said, "so I ain't going to try. Somebody broke into Mrs. Jenkins' house yesterday afternoon and knocked her down and ransacked Liddy's room, lookin' for something. We think it was some papers Liddy had. Anyways, Liddy and me come to her place in time to scare off whoever it was. Liddy didn't go to school yesterday because she's been havin' some personal problems."

I didn't say anything about Crispen Giucy because I didn't know where he stood with Mrs. Goshorn.

"Anyways," I said, "I stayed here last night on account of her and Ada—Miss Venn—was uneasy and this mornin' she went off to school whilst Miss Doyle and me went to the train station so's she could send a wire.

"On the way back we stopped at Mrs. Jenkins' place to see how she was and she was dead."

"Dead?" Mrs. Goshorn said in a shocked voice.

"Yep. Someone choked her to death and tore her place apart. I guess they was still lookin' for whatever it was they didn't find yesterday."

"This is terrible," Mrs. Goshorn said. "Did you notify Marshal Coleman?"

"Was goin' to," I said, "but we didn't have time. We run back here to get Liddy's stuff before whoever it is who's lookin' for it could find it. We got here just in time to run him off. Afore he left, though, he taken a shot at Liddy. Hit her in the arm."

"This is terrible," Mrs. Goshorn repeated, "but it doesn't tell us where Miss Venn is."

"Ma'am," I said, "I don't like leavin' Liddy—Miss Doyle— alone. Could you stay with her a bit until I can find a doctor and send him out and tell the marshal about Mrs. Jenkins?"

"Yes," she said, "but hurry. With all this going on, I'm not comfortable here. And my children are home alone with a murderer running loose. And, besides, I have to find Ada Venn and someone to teach tomorrow if she's gone somewhere. Oh, dear. This is terrible."

She sounded like she was beginning to get hysterical. I fetched another glass of water. "Here, ma'am," I said, "drink this. You'll be all right and I'll send the doctor right away. Then you can go."

I left the house and headed for town. A lady on the street told me where the doctor's office was. He was a short, pudgy man with a big, bald head and a white goatee. The sign on his office door identified him as Dr. William Saven. I liked him because he listened and didn't ask a lot of dumb questions.

After I'd sent him on the way to Ada Venn's house I walked over to the marshal's office. I wasn't looking forward to meeting with

Coleman, not after what I'd done to him, but I didn't see as I had any choice.

Coleman was sitting at his desk doing some paperwork. He looked up when I entered. Scrambling to his feet he growled, "Damn you, Tackett. Yer under arrest."

I held my hands out, palms up in a gesture of conciliation. "Later, Marshal. Right now you got real problems."

"Oh, no," he said. "Yer the one with real problems. You can't assault an officer of the law and get away with it."

"Marshal," I said, "you got a murder on yer hands. Somebody's kilt old lady Jenkins."

That stopped him cold. "What'd you say?" he demanded.

"Somebody kilt Mrs. Jenkins," I repeated. "And it was probably the same feller shot Liddy Doyle in the arm."

"Shot Liddy Doyle!" he said and sat down again. "You better tell me what you know from the beginning. Dammit! This was a peaceful town 'til you come along."

I ignored that and went on and told him the same story I'd just finished telling Mrs. Goshorn.

When I was through he eyed me up and down. "How do I know it wasn't you killed Mrs. Jenkins?"

"Yer reachin', Marshal," I said. "If yer gonna accuse me you got to accuse Liddy Doyle, too. And how do you account for the feller who shot her?"

"Oh, hell, I know you didn't do it. I'm just sore. You come in to my town and start all kinds of trouble, then ya slug me when I'm not lookin'."

"Look, Marshal," I said, "I ain't got no grudge against you. Mebbe we can start all over."

"For now," he said. "But I ain't gonna forget that you slugged me."

"I got a couple of things to take care of," I said. "Then I'll meet you back at Ada Venn's. Oh, yeah, which way is Giucy's office?"

"Next to the hotel," he said, "but don't you go causin' trouble."

The hotel was my first stop. I checked at the desk but nobody was looking for me. Then I went up to my room and carefully opened the door. But the room was empty and nothing had been disturbed. I packed everything, which wasn't very much, into my saddlebags and taken them downstairs. I paid my bill and gave the clerk a quarter to watch my stuff until I came back.

I went outside and headed for Crispen Giucy's office. On the boardwalk just ahead of me a tall, gangly, dark-haired man wearing a dark shirt and walking with just the trace of a limp came out of an office and headed away from me. He looked vaguely familiar but I paid him no mind, set as I was on seeing Giucy. He turned in at a saloon about the time I opened a door marked Crispen Giucy, the same door the tall man had come out of, and walked in.

A middle-aged, gray-haired woman was sitting at a small desk. Behind her and to one side was a door marked "Private." There were files along one wall and another desk where no one was sitting. Two straight-backed chairs made up the rest of the furniture.

"Howdy, ma'am," I said as the woman looked up. She had a narrow face, and a pinched mouth, and heavy frown creases. She wore rimless spectacles.

"Yes?" she asked.

"Lookin' for Crispen Giucy, ma'am. He in?"

"Mr. Giucy is busy. Do you have an appointment?"

"Now that I know he's in, I do," I said, heading for the door marked "Private."

"You can't go in," she said, starting to rise.

But she was too late. I pushed open the door and walked in.

CHAPTER 5

GIUCY WAS AS I remembered him—heavyset, running just a bit to fat, dark hair, smooth-shaven, and with an arrogant expression on his coarsely handsome face. He looked up, startled, as I entered the room and started to say something, but I didn't give him a chance to do more than open his mouth. I taken three steps across the room, put my hands on the edge of his desk, and began shoving. It was a heavy desk, but I'm a big, old mountain boy with my arms and shoulders heavy-muscled from growing up swinging a pick and using a shovel in those hillside gold mines in the high Sierras.

Before he knew what was happening the back side of the desk rammed into Giucy, and his chair, with him in it, went over backwards, and in just a second he was pinned under the desk which I had continued to push until it was tight against the wall.

The noise brought in the woman from the other room. She taken one look and started to leave, but I grabbed her arm and sat her down in one of the two straight-backed office chairs and said, "Stay here, lady. You may be needed."

By this time Giucy was shouting curses and trying to push the desk off of himself with not much luck. One of his feet had come out from under the desk and I went over and put a heavy boot on it.

"Lie still," I said. "I'll let you out of there after we've talked."

51

In reply he started to curse again and then shouted in pain as I put more weight on his foot. I let up and he said, "Damn you to hell. What do you want?"

"My ma taught me not to swear in front of ladies," I said. "And there's a lady present here so watch what yer sayin'."

"I'll kill you when I get out of here," he said bitterly.

"If," I said. "Not when. You talk to me civil or you'll spend the night under there. You tell me what I want to know and I'll have you out of there in jig time."

"What do you want?" he asked.

"For one, where's Ada Venn?"

"That bitch?"

I stepped on his foot again until he hollered. "That ain't nice talk. Like I told you there's a lady here," I said. "Where is she?"

"How the hell should I know? I haven't seen her since yesterday."

"She's disappeared and I think you know where she went."

"If you have any money lying around you better look to it," he said. "She probably took it and ran."

That shook me. It was an answer I hadn't expected. He was saying Ada Venn was a thief. Also he was saying he knew a lot more about her than I thought he knew.

"Tell me about Ada Venn," I suggested.

"Let me out of here and I'll tell you all about her."

"I'll let you out," I said. "But when you get up, get up careful-like because there'll be a six-gun pointed at your gut and I got a light trigger finger."

I grabbed the edge of the desk and pulled it back toward the center of the room. Behind it Crispen Giucy pushed the desk chair to one side and struggled to his feet. I had my gun out and pointed at him, but he paid it no mind.

"Damn you," he growled. "You damn near broke my neck."

He wiggled it back and forth and around in a circle. Then he reached up with his right hand and began rubbing it. After a minute he began lowering his arm. Suddenly, a small gun, one of those little two-shot derringers, popped out of his sleeve and into his hand. Before I could move, the front end of it flowered an orange flame and something hit me in the left side of my chest and knocked me backwards. I half staggered, half ducked to one side as the gun flowered again, but this time he was in too big a hurry and I was moving and he missed me.

I steadied myself and swung my gun around on him, but he flung his arms in the air and hollered, "Don't shoot."

I forgot all about Ma. "You sonofabitch, you shot me. I oughta kill you where you stand," I snarled.

I shifted my gun to my left hand and with my right hand reached into my shirt to see how bad I was bleeding. It hurt when I touched the spot where I'd been hit but I couldn't feel any dampness and when I drew my hand out and took a quick look there wasn't no blood on it at all.

"Of all the lousy luck," Giucy growled. "I hit that damned tin badge. What the hell are you doing wearing it anyway?"

I looked down. There was a big dent right square in the middle of the badge. I looked up. "I'm a deputy sheriff," I said. "You done assaulted a officer of the law."

"So arrest me," he sneered.

"Ain't about to do that," I said. "First thing, I ain't got no key to the jail and even if I did yer flunky, ol' Marshal Coleman, would turn you loose. Besides you don't do me no good in jail. But I'm mighty riled at the way you tried to kill me so what I plan to do is beat you half to death less'n you tell me what it is I want to know. And the first thing I want to know is what you meant when you said Ada Venn might have stole my money."

"Mister," Giucy said, "I don't know if you have any money but if you do I wouldn't put it past her to steal it."

"Seems like a nice enough lady to me," I said.

"That's what my brother thought," he said. "Until she took him for everything he had. Then when he came down with consumption she sent him on to Arizona and said she'd follow him when the school year was over. But she never did. And he died out there alone. Hell of a way for a wife to treat her husband."

"Wife!" I said in surprise. "She told me she never married the feller. Never did tell me his name. Just said he got consumption and went to Arizona and died afore she could foller him there."

"His name was Ripon Giucy, named after the town we came from in Wisconsin. They decided they wouldn't tell folks they were married—it was her idea—until she quit teaching school. She said it would be better that way.

"When she sent him to Arizona she kept most of his money. Said it would be safer with her. I didn't know until after he died that he was out on the street without money enough even to rent a room. You wonder why I called her a bitch."

"You ain't much better," I said. "Tryin' to steal Liddy Doyle's half of The Wait and See mine.

"You can't prove that," he said.

"That's 'cause you got someone else doin' yer dirty work. Well, let me tell you somethin'. I've seen the feller and when I run him down—and I will—I'm gonna beat the truth out of him. Then I'm gonna turn him over to Sheriff Fothergill for killin' old lady Jenkins."

"I didn't tell him to k . . . ," Giucy said, stopping in mid-sentence and knowing he'd already said too much. "You can't prove anything," he said. "I don't have the vaguest idea what you're talking about."

"Yer a liar, Giucy," I said. "The truth ain't in you. Yer probably lyin' about Ada and I know yer lyin' about what's been goin' on. Let me tell you one thing, right now. You better hope the law gets you for this because if it don't I will and what I do to you will make the law look tame."

I turned to the woman still sitting in the chair. She was white-faced and was twisting a handkerchief in her hands. "Lady," I said, "yer workin' for a thief and a liar and a man who hires women killed. With what you know now yer life ain't worth a plugged nickel if you stay around this town. You better get out while the gettin's good."

I stomped out, slamming the door behind me.

I stood out there on the street in that hot Texas sun without any idea of what to do next. I'm no planner and I'm certainly not a deep thinker. And I sure didn't have any experience in solving crimes or tracking down criminals. I wouldn't know a clue if one rose up and bit me. But I knew I had to do something. First thing, I figured, was to go back to Ada Venn's house and see how Liddy was. The doc should have her bandaged up by now.

Down deep I was hoping Ada would be there and could explain where she'd been all day. I had liked her, and even if she had been a mite forward, there was something between us now, or maybe I felt that way because there for a few minutes last night there hadn't been anything between us.

But I knew I was fooling myself. I knew exactly where she was and where she was going and why. She was on a train heading for Denver and she was carrying the deed to The Wait and See and letters that would identify her as Liddy Doyle and let her get at the $50,000 that was in the bank in Bonanza.

With that kind of money she could go to San Francisco and live the good life. But supposing she was determined to stay in Bonanza and keep Liddy's half of the mine? There was only one way to do that. Kill Liddy before she could get to that lawyer, Kooby Rarbil, in Denver. Hadn't seemed to me that Ada was that kind of woman, but if what Giucy had told me was true I had really misjudged her. Oh well, it wouldn't be the first time I'd misjudged a woman, or a man either, for that matter.

About halfway to Ada's house I met Doc Saven and Mrs. Goshorn.

"Liddy all right?" I asked.

"She'll be just fine," the doctor said. "Bring her in tomorrow and I'll change the bandage."

"You leave her alone?"

"She said she'd be all right by herself," Mrs. Goshorn said.

"I hope so," I said, taking off at a run.

I could have saved my energy. I burst into Ada Venn's house to find Liddy curled up and asleep on the sofa. The color was back in her cheeks and she was breathing normally. She sensed my presence and opened her eyes.

"It's you," she said. "I'm so glad you're back. I can rest easy now." She closed her eyes, sighed, and drifted off again.

I sat down in the easy chair and watched her a moment. A great feeling of tenderness welled up in me. This was not only a pretty girl but also an especially nice person and somebody or two or three somebodies were out to steal her inheritance and just generally give her a bad time. Well, if I had anything to say about it they weren't going to get away with it. Billy Bob Doyle had been a friend of mine and I wasn't going to sit by and see his daughter robbed of what was rightly hers.

As I pondered, it seemed to me that the best thing to do was to see if we could beat Ada Venn to Denver and prove to Kooby Rarbil that Liddy was the rightful heir to half The Wait and See. The more I thought about it, though, the more I knew that that was only half the problem. The other half was getting her there alive.

I was certain that Crispen Giucy would try to stop both us and Ada Venn. He had at least one cold-blooded killer on his payroll— the tall, dark-haired man in the dark clothes—and probably had others at his beck and call. He himself was a dangerous man, a man totally without scruples or any sense of fair play. I had the dent in my badge to prove that.

Getting up, I went out in the kitchen and stirred the fire. There were still a few coals left and I put in some wood. It was midafternoon and I hadn't had anything to eat since breakfast. I think best with something in my stomach, or so I like to think, so I looked around to see what was available. There was a loaf of bread, a pat of butter, and the remains of a ham. There was also a cookie jar filled with cookies. I put them all on the table and went about making a pot of coffee. Then I went in to awaken Liddy.

Leaning over I shook her gently. She opened her eyes and looked sleepily up at me, her lips parted slightly. I stifled an urge to bend over farther and kiss her. Dang, I thought guiltily, last night it was Ada Venn and now here you are wanting to kiss this nice, sweet girl. Get a hold of yourself, boy.

"You need to wake up," I said. "We need to talk. We got some plannin' to do and some decisions to make. I made some coffee and put some food on the table."

She sat up, then stood up a bit shakily. I reached for her but she shook me off. "I'm just fine," she said.

Doc Saven had rigged her up a sling which she now put her arm in, adjusting it until it was comfortable. She excused herself and walked unsteadily to the hallway that led to the bedroom. In a few minutes she joined me in the kitchen. Her face was washed and she had brushed her red hair until it shone. Her emerald-green eyes were clear.

"You all right?" I asked, pulling back a chair so she could sit down.

"My arm hurts a little, but otherwise I'm fine," she said. "Doctor Saven said I shouldn't have any trouble."

"That's good," I said, "because we got other troubles and we got to get movin' afore they get on top of us."

"Did you find out what has happened to Ada?" she asked.

"Ada's part of our problems," I told her. "Her and Crispen Giucy. Both of 'em are tryin' to steal yer mine and yer money. Leastwise, that's the way it looks. I gotta hunch Ada is on her way to Denver or Bonanza right now with the deed to your half of the mine and the letter from that lawyer feller. If I'm right she's gonna try and cheat you out of yer half of the mine, or at least steal yer money and head for parts unknown.

"And I think Giucy's got the same idea. I seen a feller who looked like the man who took the shot at you comin' out of Giucy's office. I'll bet my last nickel he's the same feller who killed old lady Jenkins and ransacked her place. The only thing he could of been lookin' for was the deed to the mine."

"But why?" she asked, a perplexed look on her face. "What good would that do him?"

"Way I figure it the only reason he wanted to marry you was to get yer half of the mine. When that didn't work he decided to steal the deed. Then he could force you to sign a bill of sale for a few dollars or, more'n likely, once he had the deed he'd see that you just disappeared. Then he could forge a bill of sale and no one would be the wiser."

Liddy's face paled. "You mean he'd have me killed?"

"Or do it hisself. He's a man without a conscience. I bet anything if you looked hard enough you'd find there was some murders behind him. He ain't the kind to meet you face to face. He'll shoot you in the back or get you when you ain't lookin'. He tried to kill me today with a little hideout gun he'd got up his sleeve."

I took off the badge and showed her the dent. "Saved my life. Fothergill don't know it yet but I sure owe him."

I had piled all this on Liddy pretty fast and I could see she was having a tough time fighting back tears. When she spoke there was a quiver in her voice. "What will I do, Del? The mine isn't worth dying for. And what will I do about Ada?"

"First thing we're gonna do is see if Fothergill is back from Bountyville. I hope yer up to walkin'."

"Oh, yes," she said, smiling what she hoped was a brave smile, but not really succeeding.

We took it slow, but ten minutes later we were walking into the sheriff's office. He was back and him and Marshal Coleman were in deep conversation. It wasn't hard to figure out what they were talking about.

"Howdy, Sheriff," I said. "Miss Doyle and me need to talk to you if you got a minute."

"And I need to talk to you," Coleman interrupted. "If I understand it right you and Miss Doyle was the last two to see Mrs. Jenkins alive. I'm gonna need a statement from both of you. And furthermore, I don't want neither of you leavin' town 'til I tell you you can."

I laughed. "Just this mornin' you couldn't get rid of me fast enough."

"Been better for both of us if you'd left when I told you to," he growled.

"Marshal," I said, "even though Crispen Giucy thinks he's got you in his pocket I think yer an honest man, so I want you to hear what I got to say to the sheriff here."

He didn't say nothing but I could see he liked the idea of being thought of as honest. The funny thing is, I wasn't kidding him; I thought when it came down to having to decide between being an honest lawman or being a crook he'd choose being honest, even if Giucy didn't like it. On things that didn't matter, like trying to run me out of town, then he didn't mind doing what Giucy wanted.

Whilst he and Fothergill listened I went over all that had gone on, including my run-in with Giucy and his attempt to kill me. I taken the badge out of my pocket and tossed it to Fothergill.

"It saved my life, Sheriff—you must of blessed it before you give it to me—but I think I better resign as your deputy while the resignin' is good. Looks like me and Liddy'll be leavin' town pretty quick.

"If my hunches are right, it ain't safe for her to be alone in this town right now. Besides we got to get to Denver before Ada gets there, if that's where she's headin' and I think it is.

"Sheriff, I was wonderin' if you could look after Miss Liddy whilst I run a few errands and see about me and her gettin' to Denver."

"I'll take her home with me," Fothergill said. "Della, that's the missus, will be glad for the company."

CHAPTER 6

I LEFT THE SHERIFF'S office and headed for the depot. As I went it occurred to me that maybe I hadn't been smart talking the way I had in front of Coleman. True, I thought he was an honest man, but the fact was I hadn't anything to base my thinking on. He was known to be Giucy's man and on top of that he owed me for the sock in the jaw I'd given him earlier. And, if I was wrong about him, he could create more problems for Liddy and me before we ever left town. Well, I'd known for a long time that trouble was my middle name. I shrugged my shoulders and strode on to the depot.

The station master was just closing up and he looked up in irritation as I came in. When he saw who it was he turned away and went on about the business of closing for the night.

"Mister," I said, "I need some information."

"I'm closed," he said.

"Look, Mister," I said, "I don't want any trouble, I just need some information."

"You'll have to come back tomorrow," he said, not looking at me.

"Dang," I said, "you do make it hard on a man. Now, look. I'm not askin' no more. I'm tellin' ya. You got some information I need and you and me ain't goin' nowhere until I get it. Now do you want me to come over there and beat it out of you or are you gonna give it to me the easy way?"

"I'll have the law on you," he said, his voice rising.

"If I don't bust yer neck first," I said, heading around the end of the counter.

"All right, what is it you want to know?" he asked, seeing that I meant business.

"First, when's the next train to Denver?"

"There is no train to Denver. You have to go to either Fort Worth or El Paso. From either city there's a train to Denver."

"In that case when's the first train out of here to either place?"

"There's a train to El Paso day after tomorrow."

"Today's train. Which way did it go?"

"Fort Worth."

"Was Ada Venn on it?"

"She was."

"Well thank you, my friend," I said. "That wasn't so hard, now, was it? I 'preciate yer help."

He glared at me and didn't say anything.

I taken a silver dollar out of my pocket. "Mister," I said, "if I was to give you this could I buy a little more cooperation?"

His eyes lit up greedily. "So long as I don't break any company rules or the law," he said, his voice suddenly pleasant.

"I need to know when that train gets to Fort Worth, where the stations are along the way from Forth Worth to Denver, and how long between stations."

"I think I can help you," he said, as I tossed the dollar on his desk.

It was almost dark before I got to the Fothergill house. A pleasant-looking woman answered the door.

"You must be Mr. Sackett. Won't you come in?" she said with a smile, and stepped aside to let me enter.

"Tackett, ma'am. Del Tackett," I said taking off my hat and entering. "I come to fetch Miss Doyle."

"She's sleeping now. This has been a very difficult day for her, as you know," she said, ushering me into the parlor. "Perhaps she could spend the night here."

Fothergill looked up from an easy chair and closed the Bible he had been reading. Seeing who it was he stood up and came over and shook my hand.

"Set and stay awhile," he said. "Supper's bein' fixed and Mrs. Fothergill—Della—has already set you a place at the table."

"That's mighty kind of you, Sheriff," I said, taking a seat on the sofa. "If it ain't puttin' you out none."

"Not at all. Glad to have you. There's a basin and soap by the back door if you'd care to wash up. Then, while we're waitin' for supper you can tell me yer plans."

Taking the hint, I went out in back and washed the dirt off my face and hands and made a stab at combing my hair with my fingers. It was long and unruly but in the day and a half I'd been here there hadn't been no time to find a barber. I had managed to shave this morning, though, and that made me feel a little more kempt than I might otherwise have felt.

"If she's up to it, me and Liddy'll be pullin' out in the mornin'," I said when I'd rejoined the sheriff. "I'm gonna hire me a buckboard and see if we can beat the train to Wichita Falls. Ada has to lay over a day in Fort Worth before she can catch a train to Denver and that gives us a chance."

"What're you gonna do if you catch her?" Fothergill asked.

"Ain't got that far. Got to catch her first," I said. "I really ain't wantin' to cause her any grief. I just wanna get Liddy's stuff back from her. Dang it, I liked that woman. Why'd she have to go and steal it anyway?"

Remembering last night I thought guiltily that I'd done more than just like her. On the other hand, it wasn't me who'd gone into her bedroom.

"Some folks are just naturally dishonest, other folks get desperate," the sheriff said, interrupting my thoughts.

Then he changed the subject. "You might do better takin' the stage to Wichita Falls. One leaves out of here first thing in the mornin'."

Just then Liddy walked into the room. Even with her arm in a sling and looking a little pale, she was a strikingly attractive woman. It didn't hurt neither that she was wearing a dress that showed off a figure worth showing off. Before she could sit down Della Fothergill called us to supper.

She surprised me with a roasted chicken, mashed potatoes, and cooked carrots. They were, she announced proudly, all from her kitchen garden except for the chicken which came from a coop out by the barn.

"Thanks to Della we eat well, even on lawman's pay," Fothergill said, nodding at his wife. "I hope we do as well when I go to preachin' full time."

"We will, Father, we'll do just fine," Della Fothergill said. "You've always said the Lord takes care of his own, and you are certainly one of those."

"I try," Fothergill said. "But sometimes I wonder if being a lawman is a proper thing for a born-again Christian."

"Seems to me the Lord wouldn't have it no other way," I said. "Ain't no room for churches in a land without laws, even if it means bringin' the law at the end of a gun."

"You're right, of course," he replied. "But the violence sometimes disturbs me, even when I know there is no alternative. As an individual I can turn the other cheek but when the safety and rights of others are at stake I have to do whatever is necessary even if it goes against my religious convictions. Shall we say grace?"

The supper was as good as it looked, including the dried peach pie for dessert and the coffee. I had two big slabs of the pie and three cups of coffee. Afterward I offered to help Mrs. Fothergill with the dishes but she would have none of it so me and Fothergill went back into the parlor and let the womenfolk clean up.

He broke out a couple of small Mexican cigars and offered me one. Ordinarily I'm not much of a smoker but after a big dinner a cigar always tastes good to me so I taken it and lit up. They were strong but they tasted good.

"Maybe we ought to go out on the porch," Fothergill said. "Della doesn't much like the smell of cigar smoke."

On the porch I remembered something.

"I thought you said you had kids."

"We do. Two of 'em. Frank and Kate. They're staying at the neighbor's tonight. Thought it might be better that way."

"Sorry to put you out, Sheriff," I said. "I'll pick Liddy up first thing in the morning and take her back to Ada's house to pack for the trip. I'll be stayin' at Ada's tonight and I'll pick my gear up at the hotel on the way to the stage station."

Fothergill told me it wouldn't be necessary for me to pick Liddy up. He would bring her to Ada's in plenty of time for her to pack and get to the stage station.

We finished the cigars and went back inside where we took a minute to explain tomorrow's plans to Liddy. It was all fine with her but she had the same question Fothergill had had.

"What will we do if we find Ada?" she asked.

"I'll figure that out when we find her," I answered. "I don't want to hurt her or nothin'. I just want yer stuff back."

I said good night and headed for Ada's, aided by the light of a nearly full moon. When I got there Henry came bounding down from the porch to meet me. When I opened the gate and went in he tried to lick my hand. I patted him on the head.

"Looks like Ada went off and left ya," I said. "Where ya been all day?"

Henry didn't respond, but he stayed close by my side as I walked up to the house. Inside I found a lamp and lighted it with one of those big, wooden farmer matches that I always carried. Henry followed me into the kitchen and I got him a bowl full of water and put some chunks of bread and a couple of slices of beef on a plate. He was hungry and went right after it without ever bothering to say grace.

"Henry, old boy," I said, "if Ada's gone off and left you I'll see if I can find a home for ya with the Fothergills."

He paid no attention, just kept on eating.

I found and lighted another lamp and made a tour of the house. The intruder had torn up Ada's room but the rest of the house hadn't been touched.

I went back and got Henry and put him outside. "You holler if anyone come around," I said. "I'm getting some sleep."

I was up at first light and Henry and me had eaten and I'd had a couple of cups of my coffee, which wasn't much compared to Della Fothergill's, when the sheriff and Liddy walked up.

Liddy went to pack a carpetbag and Fothergill was turning to go when I told him about Henry.

"Ada's went off and left Henry, here," I said. "I hate to just leave him here. Maybe you and Della would feel better if you had a watchdog around. Henry's a good one."

"I'll take him along," he said. "I've had a hankering for a dog, so if Della likes him I'll keep him. Otherwise I'll try and find him a home."

"Thanks," I said. "After all, he's one of God's critters, too."

Fothergill smiled. "Amen," he said. "Who knows, you come back here and maybe I'll convert you."

"Some folks got more sins than can be forgave," I said.

We shook hands and he taken off with Henry at his heels, almost as if he knew he'd found a new home and a new master.

I went back inside and poured me another cup of coffee. About then Liddy came out of the bedroom toting a carpetbag. I swallowed the last of my coffee, hoisted the bag onto my shoulder, and we walked the short distance to the stable where Old Dobbin had been loafing away the last two days.

He was glad to see me and showed it by nuzzling me in the neck. I threw the saddle on that big bay gelding, paid off the hostler, and the three of us walked on to the stage station. Abilene was the starting point for the trip to Wichita Falls and a few minutes after we arrived the six-horse stage pulled up outside the station.

I went out and got Old Dobbin and tied him behind the stage. I didn't have no plan to come back to Abilene and I sure had no thought to leave Old Dobbin behind; we'd been together too long. As I went to go back inside a man coming down the boardwalk turned and went in the door in front of me. He was tall and lanky and had dark hair and he walked with just the trace of a limp.

He was wearing a six-shooter low on his right thigh. There was no doubt in my mind that he was the man I'd seen leaving Crispen Giucy's office, but whilst he might have been the man who shot Liddy and ran, I had no way of knowing for sure. I had never gotten a good look at that feller.

My impulse was to grab him and demand to know what he'd been doing yesterday when Liddy had been shot. So I did just that. I followed him through the door, grabbed him by the shoulder, and swung him around. Before he could move I taken him by the shirt front, hoisted him onto his tiptoes, and marched him backward until I had him shoved against the wall.

For the first time I got a good look at him: Black, greasy hair, a narrow face with a hawk nose and a scattering of blackhead pimples on either side of it, a scraggly black mustache, narrow brown eyes that now were glaring at me, and a wide, thin-lipped mouth.

"All right, Mister, what was you doin' at Ada Venn's house yesterday mornin?," I rasped.

"Go to hell. I don't know what yer talkin' about," he snarled back.

"I think you do," I said. "And if I have to beat the truth out of you I will."

"I'll kill you," he said. "You lay a hand on me and if I don't do nothin' else in my life I'll kill ya."

I dropped my hands and stepped back. "Mister, if you wasn't at Ada Venn's yesterday I apologize. But if you was—and I intend to find out—you won't have to wait long to try to kill me 'cause I'll be standin' right in front of you."

The fire had gone out of his eyes and now they were a dull, lifeless brown. "Don't you never lay a hand on me again," he said.

I turned away from him and went back to where Liddy was sitting.

"Must you always be beating up on people?" she asked disapprovingly.

"I think that's the feller who shot ya," I said. "And if I'm right he's the feller who killed Mrs. Jenkins. And if that's the case he's the feller who tore up her house and Ada's house, probably lookin' for stuff havin' to do with yer mine. On top of all this, I seen him comin' out of Giucy's office yesterday, which means he's probably workin' for him. And I thought maybe I might shake somethin' out of him but he's a tough hombre. Fancies hisself to be a bad man."

"But you didn't have any proof," she protested. "Del, you can't just go around hitting people and beating up on them."

I didn't say anything. We had a long, hard trip ahead of us and there was likely to be some real violence before it was over. Last thing I wanted to do was to get in another fight with Liddy, at least until we made sure she'd got all of what was supposed to be hers.

After a minute she said, "I'm sorry, Del. I know you're doing all of this for me and I don't know what I'd do without you."

She reached over and squeezed my hand.

The driver, who'd been having a cup of coffee, swallowed the last of it, climbed to his feet, and announced that it was time to go. Liddy and I went out and I helped her aboard and then helped a gray-haired woman who followed us out. I climbed in after them and taken a seat by the door. Two other men also climbed aboard. One, clean-shaven and running to fat, was obviously a salesman of some sort. The other man was small and weather-beaten, with a gray walrus mustache. He looked inoffensive enough until I noticed he was wearing two guns that looked like they were meant for more than show.

The driver hollered and cracked his whip and the six-horse team was off at a gallop. I taken a minute to look around at my fellow passengers. The elderly lady I'd helped aboard was sitting on the far side of Liddy. The three of us were facing the front of the stage. The other two men were sitting across from us, the drummer facing the women and the man with the guns facing me.

Something was wrong. I puzzled a moment and then it came to me. The man I thought had shot Liddy was not aboard. Where was he? It was possible he was riding outside with the driver but it wasn't likely. Thinking about it I didn't remember him leaving the station with the rest of us. That was odd. What reason could he have had for being there? Was he there to see someone off or was he checking up on us for Giucy. The latter seemed most likely.

We were a quiet bunch. The men across from us each nestled into his own corner and promptly went to sleep. The woman next to Liddy did the same. That left Liddy and me. We talked in desultory fashion for a few minutes. She asked if I thought we'd get to Wichita Falls in time and I said I sure hoped so. After that there wasn't much to say and pretty soon she, too, had nodded off.

I pulled my hat down over my eyes and tried to do the same. It wasn't long, though, before the jolting of the stage kind of rocked her my way and her head flopped over on my shoulder. Carefully I eased my arm around her to hold her steady. I looked over at her but all I could see was her red hair and lower down the soft swell of her bosom. I leaned back contented-like and joined the rest of the travelers in slumberland.

The morning passed slowly. A couple of times the drummer tried making conversation but no one wanted to talk.

Once he got out a cigar but before he could light it the middle-aged woman opened her eyes and said, "Young man, it is not proper to smoke those vile things in the presence of ladies."

"Sorry, ma'am. I wasn't thinking," he said sheepishly. He chewed on it for a brief time but eventually put it back in his vest pocket. As he did so his coat came open a bit and I caught a glimpse of a shoulder holster. It wasn't often that traveling salesmen carried weapons and the fact that he did made me take another look at him. His face was bland and his hands were smooth but what I'd taken for softness now seemed to be pretty solid. He was heavy, all right, but I was willing to bet now that there was solid muscle under that layer of fat. I'd seen men like that before. They look soft but when you tangle with them you find that their softness is an unpleasant illusion; they move quick and hit hard and your own punches bounce off of them like hitting a rubber ball.

Around noon we pulled into a stage station. In answer to a question from the drummer we'd come about twenty-five miles. At this rate it would be two full days before we pulled into Wichita Falls. While we ate I mulled over the situation. If we missed Ada Venn there we'd be at least three days behind her getting into Denver and by that time she could easily have taken the $50,000 and headed for parts unknown.

Maybe, I thought, the best thing to do was to leave Liddy to come in on the stage whilst I taken Old Dobbin and hightailed it to Wichita Falls as fast as I could. I could sure get there by tomorrow night, in time to meet Ada's train, especially if I could swap horses down the road a mite.

While I was thinking it over Liddy excused herself and went to freshen up and I wandered outside. The drummer had already eaten and was lounging on a bench next to the building smoking his cigar.

"Smells good," I said.

He reached inside his vest and pulled one out. "Like one?"

"I wouldn't wanna take yer last . . ."

"I have more in my luggage. They're one of my few luxuries. I order them from back East but they're made in Cuba."

I reached out my hand and taken it. It was dark tobacco, moist like it had just come out of a humidor and it had a mild tobacco scent. He handed me a little penknife and I cut off the end, put it in my mouth, and rolled it around gentle-like. Then I taken out one of my farmer matches, scratched it on my pant leg, lit the cigar, and sucked in a lungful of smoke. Like I say, I never was much of a smoker but once in a while there's nothing better than the taste of a good cigar and this was a good cigar.

I took it out of my mouth and looked at it thoughtfully. "I owe you," I said.

"My pleasure," he said. "You going through to Wichita Falls?"

I nodded. "I'm escortin' the young lady there. We got to meet the train comin' in from Fort Worth but at this rate we'll miss it."

"No way to get there any faster?" he asked.

"I could make it in time on Old Dobbin there," I said, indicating Old Dobbin whom I'd watered and given a bit of hay and retied to the stage, "but the lady has a hurt arm and ain't up to that long a ride."

"Look," he said. "I know who you are. A man back in Abilene told me you're a Sackett and that's good enough for me. I've seen one or two of your kinfolk in action and they've always been on the right side of any row I know of. I'd be honored to look out for the lady until the stage gets to Wichita Falls if you want to ride on ahead.

"By the way, my name is Morgan Adams. I do a little work investigating fraud for an insurance combine."

I started in to correct him on who I was, like I had to do most everywhere I went. The Sacketts had come from the Tennessee hills and there was members of the family all over the West, but I was the only Tackett I knew of and folks were always confusing me with them. But suddenly I thought better of it. He'd help me if he thought I was a Sackett but I didn't know what he'd do if he found I was just Del Tackett, wandering cowboy and jack-of- all-Western-trades. I'd punched cows, worked in mines, driven stage, and for a short time had worn a badge. But I wasn't no Sackett and didn't even consider myself in their league.

I reached out and shook his hand. "Name is Del," I said. "Yer mighty kind. I'll find the lady and tell her what we're doin'."

Inside I found Liddy and taken her into a corner where I quickly explained the situation. Without hesitation she agreed that we had no other choice.

"Just remember that my name is Sackett," I said. "He's doin' this because he thinks I'm one of them Colorado gunfighters. I'll explain it to him when you get to Wichita Falls and make it up to him some way."

About then the stage driver, a tough-looking man with a face wrinkled beyond his years, hollered out that it was time to go.

I taken Liddy outside and introduced her to Morgan Adams. Then I untied Old Dobbin, swung into the saddle, and taken off at a gallop for Wichita Falls.

CHAPTER 7

TWENTY MILES DOWN the road from the stage station Old Dobbin, with me in the saddle, trotted into the little town of Anson. The first building we came to was the livery stable. Out in back of it was a corral with half a dozen horses in it. In front an old man with a scraggly tobacco-stained beard was sitting in an old straight-backed chair which he had tilted back against the side of the stable.

He spat a load of tobacco juice as I rode up. "Cost ya two bits a day to stable yer hoss."

"Ain't lookin' to stay, pop. Was wonderin' if you had a horse fer sale."

He jerked a thumb toward the corral. "Just that bunch back there. Any one of 'em'll cost ya twenty bucks."

"How much if I bring him back?"

"If he's sound I'll buy him back fer ten."

I dismounted and tied Old Dobbin to a hitching post and went and looked at the horses in the corral. One of them, a big line-backed roan, taken my fancy.

Whilst I was switching my saddle onto the roan the old man said, "I told the other fella that was the best horse I had but he said he preferred an Appaloosa that was there."

"What other feller?" I asked in surprise.

"Skinny, greasy-lookin' fella. Rode in a couple of hours ago. Said he was headin' fer Wichita Falls. Left his horse here. Said he'd pick him up in a few days. Seemed like he was in a mighty big hurry."

"Dang," I said, "no wonder he wasn't on the stage."

"You say somethin'?" the old man asked.

"Talkin' to myself," I said, handing him a double eagle gold piece. "Thanks fer the information."

I picked up Old Dobbin's lead rope, climbed on the roan, and dug in my spurs. He taken off so fast that Old Dobbin didn't have a chance to move and the lead rope was yanked out of my hand, and before I could let go I was dang-near yanked out of the saddle.

Cursing a blue streak, in spite of Ma's objections, I reined the roan up short, swung around and picked up the lead rope, and started off at a sedate trot. Behind me I could hear the old man cackling.

It didn't seem likely I could make up two hours on the dark-haired man before we got to Wichita Falls, but I was going to try. My hope was that he figured all he had to worry about was beating the train to town. As far as he knew I was on the stage with Liddy Doyle and he'd beat it there by at least a day.

I kept the roan at an easy trot for an hour, then slowed him to a walk for another hour and trotted him again until it began to get dark. As the sun went down I began keeping an eye out for a camp fire but it wasn't until the moon was coming up that I spotted it ahead and off the road a ways.

I pulled the roan up and dismounted, tying both him and Old Dobbin to a scrub tree just off the trail. I fished a pair of moccasins out of my saddlebags and put them on, tying my boots together and hanging them over the saddle. I didn't aim to announce my presence to Greasy-Hair until I had him in my sights.

Walking carefully so as not to make any noise I eased up close to the camp fire which had been built on the edge of a small clump of scrub oak. The fire seemed to have burned down a mite, but the thing that surprised me was that there wasn't nobody there. But then off to the side I saw what I took to be a man wrapped in a blanket. He looked to be asleep.

I taken my gun from its holster and tiptoed over to the sleeping figure. I was just squatting down to jab my gun in his ribs when a voice in back of me said, "Drop yer gun, whoever you are, and don't move or yer a dead man."

I recognized the voice. It was Greasy-Hair. I stood up slowly and carefully and turned around. He stared at me in surprise.

"Yer supposed to be on the stage," he said.

"Too slow," I said.

"You should've stayed on it," he said. "It don't look now like yer ever gonna get there."

I tried to change the subject. "Who's yer friend?" I asked.

He walked over to the blanket and kicked it. "Just leaves and dirt," he said. "You fell for one of the oldest tricks in the book. I didn't think you was that dumb."

"I didn't figure you was that smart," I answered.

"It don't matter what you figure," he sneered, " 'cause yer a dead man."

"Yer loss," I said.

"What d'ya mean by that?"

"Ada or Giucy may get the $50,000 but Giucy ain't gonna get Liddy's half of the mine because Ada ain't got the deed."

All of a sudden he was interested. "Who's got it?"

"Me," I lied, showing him how dumb I was. "And I'll let ya have it if ya turn me loose."

"Where is it?" he demanded.

"I got it," I lied again. "Turn me loose and I'll give it to ya."

"You got a deal," he said.

But I knew what kind of a deal I had. Deed or no deed I was a dead man. All I could do was stall for time.

"Tell me somethin' first," I said. "Did you kill that old lady?"

He laughed. "Naw. Giucy done it. He was with me when we went back to search her house. I'd knocked her out again. Second time in two days, but she come to and seen him and recognized him. So he strangled her and then went on back to his office while I went over to the other place where you found me. I should've killed ya then.

"Now gimme that deed and I'll turn ya loose."

"I got it in a pouch strapped to my leg," I said leaning over slow and careful-like. In the dim camp fire light he couldn't see much as I pulled up my pant leg until it cleared the haft of my hideaway knife. As soon as it was clear I grabbed it and in one motion flipped it underhand at him.

He seen it coming and tried to avoid it, stepping backward and to one side, right into the camp fire. At the same time he shot. But he was off balance and moving and I was ducked low and heading toward him. His bullet went over my head as I went at him. By this time he was feeling the heat from the fire and as he danced out of it I hit him in the midsection with my shoulder and he went over backward with me on top of him. He hit the ground with a grunt and his gun went flying. I grabbed him with both hands by the throat and banged his head half a dozen times on the ground until he went limp.

I climbed off of him and looked around for my gun and knife. I saw the gun and went over and picked it up and then went back and looked down at him. He was still unconscious and then I saw my knife. It was sticking out of his left shoulder. It was too high to have killed him but it would put him out of commission for awhile. Besides, a puncture wound like that could get infected easy. At least I hoped so.

I yanked the knife out of his shoulder and wiped it off on his shirt. For a minute I thought about helping him and then I remembered that he'd stood by and let Giucy choke that old lady to death and that he'd have killed me if I hadn't had my knife.

But then I thought about Charlie Fothergill. I knew what he'd do; he'd doctor his wounds and then take him to jail. Might even pray over him. Me, I wasn't going to do any of that. If he lived I knew I'd have to face him again someday. If he died, well, I didn't much care. Main thing was that right now he was one less gun to have to worry about.

I trotted back to my horses, changed my moccasins for my boots, and headed down the trail toward Wichita Falls. It was late when I found a camping spot by a small stream. I watered the horses, but didn't bother to build a fire. I spread out my ground sheet, unrolled my blankets, crawled between them, and quick-like drifted off to sleep.

It was still dark when I awoke. I put together a tiny fire that I knew couldn't be seen from the trail and made myself some coffee. First I'd had since yesterday noon. It was strong, the way I like it, and it tasted good. I ate a chunk of stale bread and chewed on a piece of beef jerky whilst I saddled Old Dobbin. I'd ride him this morning and switch to the roan after noon. If nothing went wrong I would make Wichita Falls by late evening. The train from Fort Worth was also due in about then and would lay over until morning. That would give me a chance to find Ada Venn.

The roan was a sturdy horse with a lot of stamina and go, so when I switched to him it didn't slow me down none.

About noon I came up to a lonely stage station being run by a man and his wife. They were ranching on the side and the woman had put in a kitchen garden. She fed me a beef stew filled with carrots and potatoes and onions, best I'd had in a long time. She protested when I offered her a dollar but she took it when I told her I might need a free meal the next time I came by. Her husband told me it was about 40 miles to Wichita Falls.

This was flat country like it had been all the way from Abilene so I made good time and rode into Wichita Falls just after dark.

It was a railroad town and was lively and growing. I found a stable where I rubbed the horses down and forked them some hay.

I gave the hostler 50 cents and asked if there was a hotel in town. There was three, but he told me the Wichita Falls House was the best. I decided I'd stay there and also start my hunt for Ada there.

The Wichita Falls House was a three-story building. It had a good-sized lobby and its own dining room. I got me a room on the second floor but before I headed upstairs I asked the clerk if the train from Forth Worth had come in.

"A couple of hours ago," he said.

"Anyone check in since then?"

He picked up the register and looked at it. "Two men and a woman, before I came on duty," he said.

"Woman got a name?"

He studied the register for a minute. "Mrs. Ona Zirra. Sounds Spanish, don't it?"

"Could be," I said noncommittally. "She come down since she checked in?"

"Not since I been on duty."

I tossed a dollar on the counter. "Any woman comes downstairs, remember what she looks like and try to see what direction she goes in. I'll be down directly."

I taken my key, picked up my saddlebags, and headed upstairs. There was a basin and a pitcher of water in the room. I washed up in a hurry and went back downstairs. The clerk beckoned me over.

"A lady come downstairs just before you. Kind of tall and slender. Had dark brown hair. She went into the dining room."

I thanked him and strolled over to the dining room door and looked in. The only woman in the room was seated at a table by the wall with her back to me. She had brown hair.

I walked up to her table and tapped her gently on the shoulder. "Howdy, Ada," I said. "Mind if I join you?"

I didn't wait for her answer but pulled out the chair across from her and sat down. She was a cool one. She never blinked when she saw me.

"Why hello, Del," she said. "What are you doing here?"

"Lookin' for you, Ada, or is it Ona?"

She smiled. "Either one, Del. I have a long trip ahead of me and it would be wonderful if you could accompany me."

"I left Henry with the sheriff," I said.

"Oh, I'm so glad. He tried to follow me but they wouldn't let him on the train. I'm glad he's all right."

"Sheriff'll be glad to give him back if you'll go back to Abilene."

"Oh," she said, "I couldn't do that. I have business in Denver."

"You give me back what you stole from Liddy and you won't have to go to Denver," I said.

"You're a very special person, Del," she said. "And I'll never forget the night we spent together. But I couldn't do that, not even for you."

"I sure had you wrong, Ada," I said. "I thought you was a pretty nice person."

Her face turned hard. "Have you ever been poor?" she demanded. "Have you ever tried to live on what they pay teachers in a small Texas town? Do you know what it's like to be over thirty and still be a single woman? Of course you don't. You have no idea. Do you know how many ways there are for a woman to earn a living in the West?

"You can be a teacher or a waitress or a whore. Sometimes I think I'd have been better off as a whore. Oh, don't look so shocked. At least I like sex. But what I don't like is dirty, stinking, unwashed men and that's what most of the men are in this country."

She stopped talking and drew a deep breath and all of a sudden I could see she was close to crying.

"I guess you can also be a thief," I said mildly.

"You're a self-righteous sonofabitch, Del Tackett," she said bitterly. "Until you've walked in my shoes, not for a mile but just for one goddamned step, don't you dare to criticize me."

"Ya stole from a friend. Ain't no excuse for that," I said roughly. "I come to get the letter back and the deed back. After I get them I don't care what you do. I ain't judgin' ya. You can go back to teachin' or join the girls on the line. I don't care."

"You'd like that, wouldn't you?" she said. "You'd really like that. Just remember, though, you'd have to pay for what you got the other night for free."

I laughed. "Be worth it," I said. "Now why don't you and me go up to yer room and get Liddy's stuff and I'll quit botherin' ya."

Suddenly she softened, reaching out and putting her hand on mine.

"You know," she said, "you're really a nice man. We'd make a good team. You're smart and tough, and I could teach you to read and write and teach you manners, how to use a knife and fork, how to treat a lady. You know, give you some polish. I know you like me. I could tell the other night and I know I could make you love me. We can get to Denver ahead of Liddy and get that money and be gone before she ever gets there. Then we could buy a ranch, or go to San Francisco, or do anything we wish. Let's do it, Del. Let's do it. We'll make a great team."

"No dice, Ada," I said. "I may be ignorant and I might not have no manners, but I can still live with myself."

She sighed. "I'm hungry. Can we have dinner first?"

Well, why not? I was hungry, too. I summoned the waiter over and we ordered. It was one of those good dining rooms you found scattered throughout the West. Usually they were run by some chef who'd come from Europe or some big hotel back East where he'd either gotten in trouble or maybe just been afflicted with the wanderlust. In my wanderings I'd run into men from many different countries, a lot of them with good educations, some of them professional men or men who knew a trade. A lot of folks in the East thought everyone in the West was a cowboy or a buffalo hunter or a poor, benighted redskin and that wasn't the case at all.

I asked the waiter about the chef and he said all he knew was that he was from Philadelphia but he didn't have any idea why he'd come West.

"Probably poisoned someone in Philadelphia," he joked.

"Well, if he does it to me I'll die happy anyways," I said.

Ada didn't say much while we were eating, nor did she eat much even though she'd said she was hungry. I wouldn't have been hungry either in her situation. Looking at her toying with her food I felt a little sorry for her. No question that what she'd said was right. Life in the West was hard on a single woman.

Of course a pretty woman like her could always get married, especially if she wasn't fussy, but she was. It was clear she wanted someone who was not only smart but also took a bath at least once a week. Can't say as how I blamed her. But, still, she had stolen from her friend, and I couldn't forgive that.

Out here in this country we often hanged men for stealing horses and cows, horses especially. You take a man's horse and you might leave him to die alone out in the middle of nowhere, of hunger or thirst or, even today, at the hand of roving Indians. Stealing Liddy's inheritance maybe wasn't the same thing but it was near enough to trouble me.

I paid the bill and we left the dining room. In the lobby, as we headed for the stairs, there were two men standing talking, and paying no mind to us. One of them was wearing a badge.

Ada stopped and said, "Please hold this a minute," and handed me her handbag. Without thinking I taken it.

Suddenly she screamed, "Give that back to me!" and yanked it out of my hands and stumbled backward to the floor.

The two talking men looked up and then strode purposefully toward me.

"What's going on here?" the man with the star demanded. By this time Ada had gotten back on her feet.

"He tried to take my purse from me," she said, her voice trembling.

"I done no such thing," I said.

The man with the badge stared at me. "The lady says ya did. I think you'd better come with me."

"You the sheriff?" I asked.

"Marshal. Now come along. Lady, you all right?"

"I . . . I think so," Ada said, her voice still shaky.

"You wanna come along and press charges?"

"Oh, no, Marshal. I . . . I'm just passing through. I'm leaving on the train tomorrow morning." She put her hand on his arm.

"If you could just keep him from bothering me until the train leaves."

That marshal fell for it. He dang near bowed as he said, "Lady, don't you worry none. This feller has found a home with me until your train is gone."

"Oh, thank you, Marshal," she simpered. "I'm so grateful. Now, if you will excuse me, I think I will go to my room. I'm feeling a little shaky."

The man with the marshal, obviously a local businessman, spoke up.

"May I escort you, ma'am?"

"You are very kind," Ada said, taking his arm. "I am Miss Zirra, Ona Zirra."

"Good night, Ada," I said sarcastically, as the two headed for the staircase.

"You comin' peacefully?" the marshal demanded.

"I ain't huntin' trouble," I said.

We walked to the jail in silence. When we got there he opened the door and shoved me inside. Keeping me in front of him, he reached down and lifted my gun from its holster and tossed it on his desk. Taking a ring of keys off a hook on the wall above his desk he herded me over to one of three jail cells, all of which were empty, unlocked the middle one, and pushed me in.

"All right, Mister," he said. "What was that all about?"

"Ya already seem to have made up yer mind," I said.

"Look you, whatever yer name is . . ."

"Tackett," I said. "Del Tackett."

"Look, Tackett, we don't cotton much to pushing women around here."

"You been had, Marshal," I said. "You been played for a sucker. I never touched that lady."

"We saw it."

"You never seen nothin'. She screamed and fell to the floor and told you I tried to steal her handbag. Tell you what, Marshal, whyn't you send a wire to Sheriff Fothergill down in Abilene and ask him about me and her? Her name, by the way, is Ada Venn. She's a schoolteacher when she ain't stealin' things."

A look of uncertainty crossed his face. "I might do that," he said. "I just might do that."

He turned and stomped out the door.

I looked around the cell. Wasn't much there. A cot with a thin mattress and one blanket and a tin pot with a lid on it. I went over and sat on the cot. Dang! It looked like I was stuck here at least until the train left. Wasn't no way the marshal could get a wire back from Fothergill before noon tomorrow. By then Ada would be long gone.

It had been a long day. I shrugged wearily, pulled my boots off, and lay down on the mattress, trying hard not to think about bedbugs, them flat little critters that live in the seams of mattresses and come out at night and suck your blood, leaving red welts at each place they stop. A man is better off sleeping out in the open on the hard ground. Whilst I was thinking that I drifted off to sleep, just like my conscience was clear.

CHAPTER 8

I DON'T LIKE JAILS. I don't like the bedbug-infested mattresses. I don't like the slop buckets, or the lousy food. Most of all, I don't like being locked up. It ain't fittin' for a free-born American to be locked up, especially if he hasn't done nothing wrong, and this was one time I hadn't.

When the marshal came in the next morning I was up and pacing the floor.

"Sleep well?" he asked.

"This ain't the best hotel I ever stayed in," I said. "Marshal, you send that wire to Sheriff Fothergill in Abilene like I asked?"

"Sent it last night," he said. "Figure to hear back by noon if he's in town. Meantime, I'm gonna turn you loose as soon as the train leaves. That should be about ten o'clock. I'll expect you to stay around town, though, 'til I hear back from Fothergill."

"Yer making a big mistake, Marshal," I said. "You got to keep Ada—Ona she's callin' herself, only her real name is Ada Venn—you got to keep her from catchin' that train."

"Sorry, son," he said. "She hasn't broken any laws here. I don't have any reason to hold her. I'm goin' to get me some breakfast. I'll send someone over with some for you."

He turned and went out the door.

I was looking out the window at that little tent of blue that prisoners call the sky, and at the far distant horizon, and I was beginning to feel penned in, which I was, when I heard the door from outside open. Expecting it was my breakfast, without turning around I said, "I hope the coffee is hot."

"I didn't bring any coffee, Del," Ada Venn said.

For just a flash I was angry. But by the time I turned around I could see the humor in the situation and I was grinning.

"You got me good, Ada."

She was standing just inside the door with a carpetbag in one hand. I crossed the cell and looked at her through the bars. She looked a little tired but she was still a handsome woman. She set the carpetbag down and came over to where I was holding onto the bars and put a warm hand on mine.

"That wasn't very nice of me. But I just couldn't let you stop me. You can understand that, can't you? This is the only chance I'll ever have to live the life of a lady. Please say you understand."

"It ain't how much money you got that makes you a lady," I said. "My ma was a lady every day of her life and she never had a extra penny. She made a bare livin' pannin' gold up there in the high Sierras with all them rough miners, but she was a lady and she made them miners treat her like one."

"I guess you won't ever understand," she said. "Well, I'm sorry about that and I'm sorry I had the marshal put you in jail. And I guess this is goodbye."

She reached up and pulled my head close to the bars and, standing on her tiptoes, she kissed me hard on the mouth. Then she picked up her bag and went out the door. I wiped my mouth. I hadn't had breakfast but the kiss tasted pretty good. I knew she was a thief and I knew she was a mite free with her favors, but dang, I did like that woman.

She'd been gone but a minute when a young woman arrived with a tray on which was my breakfast. It wasn't too bad, a stack of pancakes, a slice of ham, and a mug of steaming hot coffee. She set the tray next to the bars and left in a hurry without saying a word. I could understand why; I must of looked pretty rough, what with needing a shave and a haircut and a bath.

It must of been midmorning when I heard the train whistle twice and I knew it was leaving town with Ada Venn aboard. It wasn't long after that until the marshal came in. He had a piece of paper in one hand and the keys to the cell in the other.

"I have a wire here from Fothergill down in Abilene," he said, unlocking the cell door. "He vouches for you and asks me to hold that Venn woman, but I can't do that, can I, now that the train's gone?"

"I guess not, Marshal," I said, taking my gun belt off a wall hook and buckling it on. "But know that you just helped a thief to escape."

He shrugged. "She didn't commit any crimes in my town. What she done in Abilene isn't any real concern of mine."

I went out the door without saying anything further and headed for the depot. The station master was a pleasant-looking, freckle-faced man with blue eyes and sandy hair.

"Howdy," he said, looking up as I entered. "What can I do for you?"

"Howdy," I said in return. "That train that just left, was that the train to Denver?"

"Yep," he said, "but it'll be a while gettin' there."

"How's that?" I asked, feeling just a tiny ray of hope.

"Cloudburst up the line about a hundred miles washed out a section of track. Take a few days to get a crew down there and get it repaired."

"What'll they do with the passengers?"

"It's workin' out pretty good. Train from Denver is due to get there sometime late tomorrow. They'll take the Denver passengers and put 'em on the Fort Worth train and switch the Fort

Worth passengers to the Denver train and send both of 'em back to where they come from."

"Thanks, Mister," I said. "You been a big help."

I hurried to the hotel to get my saddlebags and check out. Dang, I thought ruefully, thanks to Ada I hadn't gotten even one night in that hotel bed. I scratched myself idly under my left arm. Dang bedbugs, and I didn't even have time to get any washed out of my clothes that might be hiding there. Well, anyway, they weren't as bad as body lice. I'd picked up some of them once, I won't say how, and had a hard time getting rid of them. Horse doctor I knew finally fixed me up with some kind of oil that smelled me up so bad I was embarrassed to go to town but at least it killed the little critters.

I headed for the stable to get Old Dobbin and the roan. I had a long ride ahead of me, about a hundred miles, and they'd just come off of an even longer ride. Wasn't nothing I could do, though. I had to catch that train before they transferred the passengers to the Denver train.

I paid off the stableman, including the price of a small sack of oats that I tied behind my saddle which I had slapped on the roan. He was the freshest, since I'd ridden Old Dobbin the last 25 miles yesterday. We taken off at a trot on a trail paralleling the tracks.

I had traded my boots for my moccasins and after riding about 10 miles I dismounted and ran for half an hour with the horses trailing behind me. From time to time I was delayed by a wash or arroyo which intersected the tracks. The railroad engineers had built bridges over them but often there was no easy trail crossing them.

Sometime after noon we came to one such arroyo which the railroad bridged but the trail didn't. Instead the trail veered away from the tracks a good half mile before it finally slanted down to the bed of the arroyo and up the other side. When I reached the bottom I turned up it, looking for a bit of shade where I could rest the horses for a spell. Around a slight bend, just out of sight of the bridge, I found what I was looking for, an overhang that provided ample shade for the horses and me.

I wasn't the first person to use it. There were signs of old camp fires and one that looked new. Dismounting, I took a twig and stirred it around in the ashes. They were still warm. I was curious. Who could have been down here and why? There were no ranches nearby and the trail alongside the railroad tracks was seldom used, largely because it had to cross numerous arroyos and dry washes, some of which, like this one, were steep-sided and very deep.

I'm not much of a tracker but nevertheless I taken a minute to look around. As near as I could make out there'd been two people there, or at least two horses. They'd come down the wash from the same direction I'd come and they'd gone back the same way. Or had they?

The more I looked the more it seemed to me that only one horse had gone back toward the railroad. What had become of the other horse, or was it the other horse and rider? Suddenly, I got a spooky feeling. What if one man had stayed behind to see if they'd been followed? What if, right now, he had me in his sights?

Almost without thinking, I turned and dived behind a large rock, hauling my gun from its holster at the same time, and expecting any second to hear the sound of a shot echoing through the arroyo. Nothing. The place was quiet as a church in the middle of the week.

I lay there for several minutes, not moving, hardly breathing. Then I tried an old trick. I stuck my hat over the barrel of my six-gun and raised it slowly above the rock. Still nothing. I looked at Old Dobbin and the roan, standing idly where I had tied them to the root of a big, old tree trunk that had washed down from somewhere during one of those flash floods that sometimes hit this country. Shucks, I thought, if there was something out there they ought to be acting at least a little bit nervous.

Shoving my gun back in its holster I stood up feeling a little sheepish and a bullet smacked into the side of the rock just an inch below my belly and caromed off across the arroyo. I hit the ground again like I'd been shot, with the sound of the strange six-gun ringing in my ears and echoing up and down the wash.

I let out a groan like whoever it was had hit me. But if he was fooled he wasn't taking no chances because I didn't hear another sound. The shot had come from farther up the arroyo so, gun in hand, I eased around the side of the rock away from where it had come from—and came eyeball to eyeball with a coiled rattlesnake.

Without thinking I shot his head off. My shot brought answering fire from the strange gunman. His bullet came too close, chipping off a corner of the rock and splattering me with tiny fragments.

I looked around and came to the reluctant conclusion that I was fair trapped. There was no cover between me and the horses. And once away from the rock there was no cover toward the tracks until you reached the bend which was a good hundred yards away. I thought about running for it but one thing I wasn't was faster than a speeding bullet.

It looked like the only thing I could do was wait until dark which was still several hours off. In the meantime there was nothing to prevent the stranger from climbing the side of the arroyo and circling behind me. From up on top of the bank I would be a sitting duck. Another thought hit me, too, that I didn't like at all. What if he just shot Old Dobbin and the roan and left me on foot? Then I would be at his mercy.

The situation being what it was I done the only thing I could think of. I hollered out, "Yer shootin' at the wrong man, dang it."

There was no answer. I lay there watching the minutes drag by and every now and then sneaking a look around the rock. I don't know how long I'd been lying there but I'd judge at least an hour when I heard one of the horses snort. I taken a quick peek around the edge of the rock to see what had spooked it. It wasn't what, it was who. My greasy-haired friend had showed up again. He was walking, or rather staggering, toward the horses. He was carrying his six-gun but it was dangling by his side. Before he reached the horses he stumbled and fell. For a moment he struggled to get to his feet but then lay still.

I climbed to my feet and moved slowly and carefully toward him, but he didn't move. When I reached him I kicked his gun out of his hand, then leaned down and rolled him over on his back. I could see now what his trouble was; he'd been shot in the chest. If some people are born losers it was beginning to look like he fit the description. Not two days ago he'd gotten in the way of my knife and now today he'd stopped somebody's bullet.

He wasn't dead but he was a mighty sick man. It was almost a miracle that he'd been able to shoot at me and it was easy to see why he'd missed. I fetched my canteen from my saddle and lifted his head up and poured some water into his mouth. It brought him around. He opened his eyes and stared up at me. He wasn't afraid. He may have been a loser and an evil man but there was no fear in him.

"Howdy, Tackett," he whispered. "You got yer chance now to finish what you started. Ya better take it."

"Hell, I don't wanna kill ya, man," I said, "but I won't mind leavin' ya here to die if ya don't tell me what this is all about."

"Don't matter none to me what ya do, Tackett. I'm dyin'," he whispered. "That sonofabitch shot me and shot my horse. Left me here to die. When I spotted you I figured I could shoot you and get your horses and mebbe get back to Wichita Falls and find a doc. Didn't work that way. I couldn't hold my gun steady."

He stopped and lay back and I lifted his head again and gave him another swallow.

"Who shot ya?" I asked.

"Giucy," he said so low I could barely hear him. "Said he didn't need me no more. Said I . . ." He stopped talking for a minute then without warning sat straight up. "Mother," he cried out and fell back on the ground. I didn't have to look twice to know he was dead.

I didn't have no shovel to bury him with and I didn't want to take him with me because I was going to need both horses if I was to get to the washout before the Denver train started back. I dragged his body over to the other side of the wash where the bank was steep and after going through his pockets, managed to cave a little dirt on top of him, enough, I hoped, to keep the varmints off of him.

He didn't have nothing of any consequence on him, a double eagle and some change, a sack of tobacco and a Barlow folding knife. I kept the money and the knife as well as his gun which, like mine, was a Colt .45. Not being a smoker, except for an occasional cigar, I buried his tobacco with him.

I decided I'd wasted too much time already to make any coffee at this hour. Instead I'd push on until dark. Quick-like I switched my saddle from the roan to Old Dobbin and headed back to the trail that would take me to the stalled trains.

It surprised and worried me that Giucy was on the trail. I hadn't expected that. I'd figured Greasy-Hair was his hired killer, but I didn't think he'd want to mix directly into the action himself.

He was a tougher man than I'd thought he was. Suddenly, I was worried about both the women who'd got involved in this situation. Where was Liddy and was she all right? Had I done right to trust her safety to Morgan Adams, a man I really didn't know at all? And what would happen to her if I was unable to prevent that lawyer, Kooby Rarbil, from turning the money she been left over to Ada Venn?

And Ada I now took to be in deep doo-doo, as my old friend, Herb Bushwalker, used to say. Herb was a man of many strange and different sayings. It came, I guess, from him having been raised in the East and going to some of those fancy Eastern schools before the wandering urge took him to Missouri, then down to the Oklahoma Territory and on to West Texas, where I first knew him. I asked him once where he got a name like Bushwalker and he explained that when his family was still in England it was one of those hyphenated names—Bush-Walker, but somewhere along the line somebody in his family decided to drop the hyphen.

I told him once a man with a highfalutin name like his ought to be president or at least a senator instead of a wandering cowboy, but he said his daddy had known a president once and had told him that anyone who wanted that job was out of his mind. Which maybe was true.

I snapped my mind back to Ada Venn. It was plain that Giucy had decided to stop her before she got to Denver. Like me he'd figured that if she got to Denver first she'd hornswoggle Kooby Rarbil out of the $50,000 and maybe even make some deal with him regarding Liddy's half of the mine. I was determined to stop Ada for Liddy's sake but I had no grudge against her. She was a desperate lady and I could understand why she was doing what she was; I just couldn't let her get away with it.

But Crispen Giucy was another matter entirely. He was a man absolutely without conscience or scruple. He'd killed his hired killer when he was of no further use to him and I was certain he wouldn't hesitate to do away with Ada if he decided that was necessary. But I was determined not to let that happen. In spite of everything I liked her. That was a real woman—smart, and tough and willing to take a chance.

Liddy, on the other hand, was sweet and a bit innocent, but she was also a little prissy, a little self-righteous. But her daddy had been a friend of mine and probably wouldn't have been killed if I hadn't gone to work there at the R Bar R, so I owed her and I was going to pay off that debt no matter what it took.

It occurred to me that I hadn't given much thought to the other reason I'd come to see Liddy Doyle, the hope that maybe she was the person who'd teach me to read. I'd never learned growing up because, though Ma knew how to read, she was too busy panning for gold along the creeks to find the time to teach me. And at night she was just too tired. Over the years I'd learned to count a little and make out a word here and there, and I could sign my name, but even that was a chore.

The fact that I was illiterate had never bothered me until a few months ago. I had gone back to the little mountain town of Lodestone where Ma and I had lived all those years because news had come to me that she had died. I hadn't seen her since I'd left home when I was sixteen, but there was always a strong love for her deep inside of me and I wanted to make sure she'd had a proper burial. She'd died as poor as she'd lived, leaving nothing behind except an old leather-bound diary that she'd kept over the years.

I'd never known who my father was or where we'd come from before Ma and me arrived in Carson City right after the War Between the States ended. We hadn't been there long before she accidently killed a man who was bothering her. The man had friends so she packed up our few belongings on a burro and walked out of Carson City and into the Sierras on the California side of the border where she lived out the rest of her life. During the years before I left home I had no idea that she'd kept a diary. Now I had it and I thought it might contain the secret of my birth and who my father was and why we'd come to Carson City.

Esme Rankin, who owned the R Bar R, had offered to read it for me but I was uncomfortable with the idea of sharing Ma's inner-most thoughts with anyone else. So I'd said thank you no. Then she offered to teach me to read, but I've a kind of stubborn pride and I didn't want to be beholden to the woman who I loved and wanted someday to marry. I figured I needed to learn to read on my own and then find out from the diary if there was any reason I couldn't marry her.

Esme understood how I felt and didn't argue when I left, just whispered, "Come back someday, Del." I hadn't answered, but I knew that someday I'd go back.

But not now, not until I'd finished what I'd gotten involved in here.

CHAPTER 9

From the looks of the sun I had about four hours of daylight ahead of me and I decided I would push on as fast as possible until the sun went down and then find a place to camp. But it didn't work out that way. I'd been riding about two hours when I topped a rise and there in front of me about a mile away was a dinky, ramshackle town, couldn't have been more than a dozen buildings.

As I got closer I could see there was a depot of sorts alongside of the tracks. Cantering into the town, I counted a stable, a saloon, a small general store, a blacksmith shop. There were half a dozen houses, shacks, really, one of which didn't look like no home. It wasn't much of a town, not a tree, not a blade of grass, just a few buildings squatting beside a dusty road that petered out into a trail on both sides.

I headed for the depot but it was shut tight so I went on to the saloon. I knew what it was because there was a sign on the front that said "Saloon." When I went in I discovered I'd been in better. The bar was built of rough lumber. The customary mirror in back of it was noticeable by its absence. There were three beat-up tables and a few rickety chairs, some of which looked homemade, and that was it.

The bartender was huge, taller than me, and he must have weighed over 300 pounds, most of it fat. His blond hair grew below his shoulders which weren't all that far down since he had no neck that I could see. He had a long drooping mustache that hid his rotting teeth until he smiled which was frequent. His pale blue eyes looked straight at me.

A single customer was sitting at one of the tables, nursing a drink. From his looks he wasn't no cowboy which meant he was a townie or else just passing through.

"Ya gotta beer?" I asked the bartender.

"Kind of," he grinned. "It ain't much but we pass it off as beer."

He reached under the counter and pulled out a brown bottle which he uncapped and shoved over to me.

I taken a swig. He was right. It wasn't much, but it was cool and wet.

"Where do I find whoever's in charge of the train station?" I asked.

He jerked a thumb at the man at the table. "That's him."

I picked up my beer and strolled over to the table.

"Mind if I join ya?" I asked, pulling out a chair and sitting down.

"Don't think it would do much good for me to say no," he said wryly.

"Lemme buy you a drink," I said. "And then maybe you can answer a couple of questions for me."

I went back to the bar. "Gimme the bottle of whatever it is he's drinkin'," I said. He reached to the shelf behind the bar and handed me a bottle. I taken it back to the table and set it in front of the station master.

"Name is Tackett," I said. "Help yerself."

He filled his glass. "Ghoti's my name," he said. "Shad Ghoti. What is it you wanna know?"

"How far up the line is the washout?"

"'Bout seventy-five miles."

"When'd the train to Denver go through here?"

"Couple of hours ago."

"Dang," I said, my heart sinking.

It was plain to me that the train would reach the washout and have its passengers transferred long before I could get there, even if I left right away. I just hoped Crispen Giucy would be too late, too.

"Feller rode in here earlier today," Ghoti said. "Big feller. Kind of heavyset. He was askin' about the train, too. He was luckier than you, though. Train hadn't got here yet. So I flagged her down for him. Nice feller. Gave me $5 to take his horse to the stable. Said he'd either come back for it or send someone."

"Dang," I said again. "When's that train comin' back?"

"Late tomorrow mornin', I imagine."

"Can ya flag it?"

"Yep."

"There a horse car on it?"

"Yep."

"I'll wanna ticket fer me and I got two horses I wanna put aboard."

"I'll take care of you in the mornin'."

"See you then, Mr. Ghoti," I said.

I paid the bartender, went out and climbed on Old Dobbin. Leading the roan I trotted to the stable where I paid the old man in charge fifty cents to rub down the two horses and feed them.

"I'll be sleepin' here tonight," I said, and asked, "Where does a body get a bite to eat around here?"

"Ain't no restaurant here," he said, "but most times you can get a meal of sorts up at the saloon."

I walked slowly back to the saloon, thinking as I went. Didn't seem to be much sense now in trying to beat either Ada or Giucy to Denver. I'd never make it. Best thing for me to do was get back to Wichita Falls and wait for Liddy to come in on the stage. Then we'd catch the next train to Denver.

But before we did that we'd wire Kooby Rarbil and warn him about Ada. Not that it would do much good. Anybody could send a wire and sign anyone's name to it. And Ada would be a convincing Elizabeth Doyle when she met with Rarbil.

I stopped in mid-stride. Maybe it wasn't when, but if. What if Crispen Giucy found her on the train and decided to make sure she never reached Denver? He could not only get rid of her, but he could also filch the papers she was carrying and then pass himself off to Rarbil as representing Liddy. Since he was a half-owner of the mine and since he and Liddy were both from Abilene he could present a pretty convincing story. Of course he would have to make certain that Liddy never met with Rarbil, either.

But killing Liddy wouldn't bother Giucy none. He'd been responsible for the death of old Mrs. Jenkins, he'd shot Greasy-Hair in cold blood, and by the time Liddy arrived in Denver he would have done away with Ada. I shivered a little bit, like somebody had walked on my grave; this was a man absolutely without conscience or scruple. Not only were Ada and Liddy in danger, but so was I. He'd kill me without blinking if I got in his way, or have it done for him, and it wouldn't matter to him if I was facing him or if my back was turned. I wondered where he'd come from and why he'd left and how many killings were in his background.

Me, I'd had my share, with both gun and knife, but I'd always done it in a fair fight and I'd walked wide to avoid it whenever I could. But there's some men kill once and after that they can't get the smell of blood out of their nostrils and the desire to kill again out of their systems. I was willing to bet that Giucy was one of them.

I walked into the saloon. Ghoti had left but the fat bartender was still there, swabbing down the bar with a damp rag.

"Heard a body could get a bite to eat here," I said.

He nodded. "Got some beans in back," he said. "And if you ain't in a hurry I can fry you up a steak."

"Sounds good," I said.

He dropped his rag and waddled toward the kitchen. "Holler if someone comes in," he said over his shoulder. "The likker business comes first."

He was back in a minute with a plateful of beans. "Steak comin' up," he said, heading for the kitchen again.

I was just finishing up the steak when a couple of cowboys walked in, looking grim. The fat man, behind the bar again, looked up. "What'll you have?"

"Last time I had a beer here it wouldn't of won no blue ribbon so make it whiskey for both of us," the shorter one said, and then asked, "Any law in this town?"

"Nuthin' closer than Wichita Falls," the fat man said. "You got problems?"

"In a manner of speakin'," the cowboy said. "We got a body outside. We gotta do somethin' with her."

Her! The word hit me like I'd been slugged in the belly. I taken a deep breath but before I could say anything the bartender beat me to it. He was full of questions.

"Where'd you find her? What happened? Where is she?"

"She's tied on a horse outside," the cowboy said. "We was comin' along the trail that follers the tracks a few miles back. Trail goes real close to the tracks there. Willie here spotted her on the other side of the tracks, lyin' in a bunch of rocks. Almost missed her.

"Hard to tell how she died. Fall could of killed her but there's marks on her throat like she might of been strangled first."

"Let's go look," the fat man said. The cowboys downed their drinks and headed outside. The fat man came from behind the bar and followed them out. I trailed behind, afraid of what I was going to see and hoping against hope that I was wrong.

I wasn't. It was getting dark but there was still light enough for me to recognize Ada Venn, even though her face was swollen and discolored.

"Damn," I muttered under my breath, forgetting Ma's opposition to swearing. "I'll kill that sonofabitch."

"You say somethin'?" the bartender asked, looking over at me. I shook my head.

"You know her?" he asked.

I shook my head again. "No."

If I'd said yes they'd have begun wondering which direction I came from and might have thought I knew more than I did. I didn't need to get tangled up in any situation where folks might add up two and two and come to the conclusion I had something to do with her death.

The fat man said, "Maybe one of you fellers would go over to the depot and roust out Shad Ghoti. Tell him to wire the sheriff in Wichita Falls that we got a dead woman here and ask him what we should do with her.

"You fellers find a handbag or anything that might tell us who she is?"

"Nuthin'," the cowboy who'd done all the talking said.

"I'll tell Ghoti," I said and headed for the depot.

I was sure Ada had been killed by Crispen Giucy. He must have spotted her on the train almost as soon as he'd gotten aboard. Then, somehow he'd lured her to a place on the train—probably between cars—where he could strangle her and dispose of her body.

At the same time he undoubtedly had managed to get his hands on the papers she was carrying, the papers that would have identified her as Elizabeth Doyle and would have given her access to the $50,000 in the bank at Bonanza.

But even though Ada was a thief and had tried to steal Liddy's inheritance she didn't deserve to die. She was a desperate woman, not an evil one. And she'd been someone special to me, even though I'd only known her a few days. Ordinarily I'm a peaceful type who goes out of his way to avoid a showdown, but as I walked toward the station I knew that this time I was going to go out of my way to have a showdown with Crispen Giucy. His sort didn't deserve to live and if the law couldn't protect folks from his kind, well, I was going to make my own law.

Ghoti was puttering around fixing himself some supper and wasn't in any hurry to send the wire.

"Won't get it 'til mornin' anyway," he said.

But he promised to send it as soon as he ate, so I wandered on back to the saloon where I did something I don't often do. I got drunk. Everything had gone wrong. I had missed the train and had no chance of getting to Denver within a week of when Giucy would get there. Ada Venn had been killed. And I was scared now for Liddy. I'd left her being looked after by Morgan Adams, who seemed like a solid man, but I didn't know him, and for all I knew he could have been in cahoots with Giucy. I'd been almost positive Giucy would put his man on the stage with us, but I'd just assumed it would be Greasy-Hair. But suppose instead it had been Adams?

Wasn't nothing I could do now until the train came back from the washout sometime tomorrow, so I sat there at one of those rickety tables and got quietly and moodily drunk. Eventually the fat bartender poured me a cup of hot black coffee and shoved me out the batwing doors. I walked unsteadily to the stable where I found a saddle blanket which I spread out in a pile of hay, fell down on it and went to sleep without even taking off my boots.

Daylight woke me up, daylight and a pounding headache. I groaned and climbed slowly to my feet. Outside I found a watering trough and doused my head in it. It didn't stop the pain but it did make the world look a little clearer. I went back and found my hat and walked down to the saloon, my head throbbing with every step. It was locked in front but I'd seen smoke coming from a stovepipe in back so I went on around to the back and knocked on the door. The bartender, wearing nothing but a pair of one-piece long johns which his huge belly had stretched almost to the bursting point, opened it and looked blearily at me.

"You got any coffee for a dyin' man?" I asked.

"Come on in," he said. "Seein' as how it's my rotgut that's got you feelin' that way, I guess I can spare a cup of coffee."

He went over and took a pot off the stove, and a mug off a shelf, and filled it from the pot. It was black and steaming but it tasted good.

"You don't look like a drinkin' man," he offered.

"Ain't, ordinarily," I said.

"That dead woman get to ya?" he asked.

"A little," I admitted. "Never like to see a woman murdered."

"'Specially if you know her," he said.

I took a sip of my coffee and didn't say anything.

He grinned at me through his rotten teeth. "Makes no difference to me. I know you didn't kill her. I saw you come in to town from the other direction."

"I could've circled around," I pointed out.

He grinned again. "You ain't that smart."

I shrugged. He was right and we both knew it.

"Yer right. I knowed her but I didn't kill her. But I know who did. Feller caught the train out of here yesterday. Ya might have seen him. Big feller. Black hair.

He nodded. "He bought a drink before the train came."

"Name is Crispen Giucy. He's a big shot down in Abilene. But he's a bad man. On his way here he shot a feller in cold blood. He's responsible for at least one other murder that I know of."

"You goin' after him?"

"Got to meet a lady back in Wichita Falls first. Then the two of us'll go on to Denver. We'll look for him there."

"Train won't be in for awhile. You want some breakfast?" he asked.

"Be grateful," I said.

He poured me another mugful of coffee and while I drank it he found some oats and made a potful of oatmeal mush. I hadn't had any of that since I left Ma and the mountains when I was sixteen. It wasn't exactly ham and eggs but it stuck to my ribs pretty good.

When I'd finished I stood up and reached for my hat. "Pay ya?" I asked.

"It's on the house," he said. "See you around."

I went back to the stable, paid off the stablehand, and threw my saddle and other gear on Old Dobbin. Straddling him and leading the roan I headed for the depot. Ghoti came out to meet me and said he expected the train within an hour or two.

It was nearly noon before it finally arrived and, in the meantime, I'd tilted a chair against the wall and dozed the morning and my headache away.

When the train came in I put Old Dobbin and the roan in the horse car. As I was walking toward the passenger car a couple of Mexicans pulled up in a wagon and unloaded a wooden box and put it in the baggage car. I didn't have to be a genius to figure out that they were sending Ada back at least as far as Wichita Falls.

At mid-afternoon, when the train arrived, the town was unchanged from what it had been two days earlier. And so was the town marshal, who greeted me as I got off the train.

"Sheriff told me yer lady friend was killed," he said. "You got any ideas about who done it?"

"You come down here just to meet me, Marshal?" I asked.

"Sheriff's tied up," he said. "So I'm doing him a favor. Makin' sure the body gets off the train. Makin' sure you know he wants to see ya before ya leave town."

"How'd ya know I was comin' back?"

"The saloon keeper up there, Fats Mann, kinda keeps an eye on things there for the sheriff. He had Ghoti send a wire."

"Ada was throwed from the train. Mebbe you ought to get the railroad detectives involved in this," I suggested.

"Already notified 'em," he said, walking away. "You be sure and see the sheriff."

I unloaded Old Dobbin and the roan from the horse car and took the two of them to the stable and then headed for the hotel where I checked into the same room I'd had, but never used, just two nights ago.

"Nice to have you back, Mr. Tackett," the clerk said.

"The stage from Abilene come in yet?" I asked.

"Yes sir. About two hours ago," he replied.

"I'm lookin' for a young lady who was on it. Has red hair. Real green eyes. She check in here?"

"Yes sir. There was a redheaded lady and an old woman checked in here together. They're sharing the same room."

That puzzled me. What was an old woman doing with Liddy? Then I remembered. There had been an old woman on the stage when we left Abilene, but Liddy hadn't known her. And besides, I'd left her in the care of Morgan Adams. Where was he? Something mighty strange was going on here.

"Anyone else check in?" I asked.

He shook his head. "Just the two women."

That puzzled me even more. If Liddy was with the old woman, where was Morgan Adams? Had he gone off and left Liddy? Had something happened to him?

The main thing, I decided, was that Liddy was all right. So the thing for us to do was to lay over here until the train came through again on the way to Denver. By then the washout should have been fixed and we should get to Denver in two or three days, if all went well. What I had to do now was talk to Liddy.

I got her room number from the clerk and went up to her room and knocked. A voice, not hers, called "Who's there?"

"Del Tackett," I called back. "I got to see Liddy Doyle."

There was a long silence, then the voice said, "Miss Doyle does not wish to see you."

That made me mad. "I got to see her," I said. "Let me in or I'll break the door down."

After a minute the door opened a crack and I could see Liddy standing there. Her face was pale and drawn.

"Go away, Del," she said. "I don't wish to see you. I have no further need for your help."

She closed the door and left me standing on the outside, feeling like a fool.

CHAPTER 10

FOR A MOMENT I had an urge to bust the door down and find out what was going on. It didn't make any sense to me that Liddy would say she didn't need my help anymore. It didn't make any sense that she was with that woman, who, as far as I knew, she'd never seen before we saw her on the stage. Furthermore, where was Morgan Adams?

Well, the train wouldn't be in for a couple of days yet which gave me time to look around. I turned and stomped downstairs and went over and asked the clerk where the sheriff's office was.

"You want the sheriff or the marshal?" he asked.

"Sheriff," I said. "I've done seen the marshal."

The sheriff's office was down and across the street from the marshal's. When I went in he was doing book work. Seems like every time I see some sheriff or marshal he's doing book work.

"Howdy, Sheriff," I said as he looked up. "Heard you was lookin' for me. Name is Tackett."

"Tackett or Sackett?" he asked, giving me a quizzical look.

"Tackett, Sheriff," I said. "I ain't no gunfighter. Just a cowhand passin' through on the way to Denver."

He was a gray-haired man, grizzled and lined from a lifetime in the sun and weather. "I've heard that line before," he said. "But some folks look like gunfighters and some folks don't. Not sure I'd bet against ya in a showdown."

I shrugged. "I try to avoid 'em, Sheriff."

"The good ones usually do," he said and then switched subjects. "What d'ya know about that dead woman they just shipped in from up the line?"

"Name was Ada Venn," I said. "You wanna know all I know?"

He nodded. So I told him how I'd met her whilst looking for Liddy Doyle, how she'd taken off with the information that could have gotten her the $50,000 that belonged to Liddy, how I'd caught her, and how the marshal had jailed me and let her go.

But I didn't tell him about the night I'd spent with her at her house in Abilene.

I told him about Crispen Giucy and Greasy-Hair and how I thought it was Giucy had killed Greasy-Hair and how I thought it was him had killed Ada also.

Maybe I should of, but I didn't tell him about Morgan Adams or about Liddy and the gray-haired old lady who were holed up in the hotel.

The sheriff—he told me his name was Smith and had always been—seemed satisfied with my answers but told me to stay around for a day or two in case he needed me. I told him I wasn't going anywhere, at least until the train for Denver came in.

As I left the sheriff's office I had a sudden thought and I turned and headed for the stage office.

"The stage that come in a little while ago from Abilene, has it gone on?" I asked the sandy-haired man behind the counter.

"This is the end of the line," he replied.

"Where can I find the driver?"

"Happens he lives here," he said and gave me directions to the driver's house. His name, he told me, was Chick Rewey.

Rewey, himself, answered the door when I knocked. He was barefooted and wearing only pants and an undershirt. He looked tired, which he should have, and was sipping at a mug of coffee.

"What kin I do for ya?" he asked.

"Tryin' to find a feller name of Morgan Adams. He was on yer stage when it left Abilene but he wasn't on it when you got to Wichita Falls."

He scratched his head idly. "Funny thing," he said, "first you dropped off at the first stop, then he dropped off at the second stop. Only thing is, you had a horse and he didn't. Couldn't figure it out. He got off the stage and never got back on. Didn't say nuthin' to nobody and I never even noticed he was gone until later."

"How far back is the station?" I asked.

" 'Bout sixty miles," he said.

I thanked him and headed back to the sheriff's office. He was still in.

"Sheriff," I said, "that stage that come in a bit ago from Abilene. There was supposed to be a feller on it name of Morgan Adams."

"Know him," he said. "Done business with him."

"Anyway, Adams got on the stage in Abilene but he never got here. I just talked to the driver and he says he got off about sixty miles back."

"So," he said indifferently.

"Don't make sense, Sheriff. He was supposed to meet me here."

"Ya think somethin' happened to him?"

"Yeah. And I wanna go find out what. Thought I ought to tell ya since you asked me to stick around."

"Still want ya to for the next couple of days."

I shrugged. "Just checkin'," I said. "See you around."

"I expect you will," he said to my back as I went out the door.

It wasn't yet dark so I headed back to the hotel and went on up to my room which was three doors down from the one where Liddy and the old woman were staying. I paused for a moment outside their door but, though there was the murmur of voices, I couldn't make out words, so I went on down to my room.

Being the careful kind I unlocked the door and standing to one side, shoved it open. Wasn't nobody there. I went on in and took a careful look around. Everything was just as I had left it, almost.

Something or someone had disturbed the pillow on the bed. I knew because when I'd dropped off my things before trying to see Liddy I'd stretched out on the bed for a minute just to get a load off my feet. Now, although the pillow was in the same position I'd left it in there was no longer an impression in it from where I'd lain my head. Wasn't nothing I could do about it now, so I plunked down on the bed, taken off my boots, and prepared to stretch out. I figured I had a couple of hours to kill until it was dark enough for me to leave town without being spotted by Sheriff Smith. Best thing for me to do in the meantime was to rest up. I had a long ride ahead of me.

I looked at the pillow again. Why would anyone have moved it and yet not disturbed anything else in the room? I shrugged and started to lie down. But then some instinct made me pick up the pillow and toss it to one side. There on the sheet was this round ball of cork, about the size of a large grape. But it wasn't made for eating; it was made for drawing blood, my blood. And whoever'd left it wasn't the tooth fairy.

Tiny needle points about a quarter of an inch long stuck out from the cork in all directions. If I'd of casually put my hand under the pillow one of those points would have stuck me and drawn blood. But there didn't seem to be any reason for that except maybe the purpose wasn't to draw my blood but to put something in my bloodstream. I knew immediately that without a doubt those needle points contained some kind of poison. I drew back in a kind of horror. I had faced death many times before and I wasn't afraid to die. But poison, administered by an unknown enemy. I shuddered. It was not the way I wanted to go.

Another thought struck me. I picked up a boot and with its sole pushed the deadly cork to one side. Then I threw back the top sheet and blanket. Sure enough, there at the foot of the bed on the bottom sheet was the twin of the cork I'd found under my pillow. That scared me more and got me to wondering where else I might find one of those things. Without touching them I managed to roll the two corks into the washbasin that had been sitting on a night-stand. Then, carefully and gingerly, I unpacked my saddlebags and unrolled my bedroll. Nothing.

I put on my boots and carried the basin down the hall and down the back stairs. Outside I found an outhouse and dumped the two corks in it. It wasn't likely they could do any damage there.

Back in my room I taken the chair and wedged it firmly under the doorknob. Then I lay back down on the bed and in a minute was sound asleep. It was dark when I awoke. Without bothering to light a lamp I pulled my boots on, buckled on my gun belt, put on my hat, removed the chair from under the doorknob, and went out into the hall. Three doors down I paused in front of the room occupied by Liddy and the old woman. But it was quiet and there was no light from under the door, so I went on downstairs.

The clerk was still at the counter so I went over to him and told him, "You see Sheriff Smith tomorrow you tell him not to fret, that Tackett said he'd be back in town before the train comes in."

I gave him a quarter, which he pocketed, and strolled over to the entrance to the dining room. A quick look located Liddy and her companion at a corner table. She saw me about the same time I saw her and a look of consternation crossed her face. Then she dropped her eyes and concentrated on her plate. Quickly I crossed to where they sat.

"Excuse me, ladies," I said, "I don't mean to bother you none."

I looked directly at Liddy. "Just wanted you to know I'm leavin' town in the mornin'. Headin' back to the R Bar R. Wanted to wish you luck."

She looked at me with dead eyes. "Thank you," she said without expression.

The gray-haired woman with her said nothing, just kept eating without bothering to look up. There didn't seem to be anything else to say; it was clear that for some reason Liddy didn't want to talk to me. It didn't make much sense but if that was the way she wanted it then so be it, at least for the time being.

"So long," I said and left. In case anyone was watching I went back up the stairs and down the hall toward my room, but I kept right on going past it and down the back stairs.

At the livery stable I had just finished saddling Old Dobbin when a soft voice said, "Goin' somewhere?"

"Hoss needs exercise, Sheriff," I said turning to face him.

"Thought I told ya to stay around," he said.

"Dang it, Sheriff," I said in exasperation, "there's somethin' strange goin' on and I got to find out what it is. I left Morgan Adams to take care of a lady name of Liddy—Elizabeth—Doyle. He was to bring her in on the stage and wait here until I got in touch with them. Instead he disappears off the stage and Liddy Doyle comes in here with some woman she never saw before she got on the stage. As far as I know anyway. And now Liddy says she don't want nothin' to do with me. It don't make sense. So I figure the first thing for me to do is find out what happened to Morgan Adams. Soon as I find that out I'll come back here. You got my word."

"Seems you didn't tell me the whole story when we talked before," he complained.

"Sorry about that, Sheriff," I said, "but when I talked to you I still wasn't sure there was somethin' wrong. I still ain't except it don't make no sense that Liddy won't talk to me. And it makes even less sense that Morgan Adams went off and left her—if he did. He didn't seem like that kind of feller."

"He ain't," Sheriff Smith said. "Told ya I know him. Tell ya what. You Sacketts got a reputation for keepin' yer word. I'll let ya go but you report back here to me in three days, hear?"

"Name is Tackett," I said.

"Makes no mind," he said. "I'll be waitin' to hear from ya."

"Sheriff," I called as he walked away, "left my bedroll and saddlebags at the hotel. Keep an eye on 'em for me, will ya?"

He waved a hand without looking back and I went on saddling Old Dobbin.

"Take care of that roan. I'll be back in few days," I said to the stablehand as I led Old Dobbin outside.

Old Dobbin was feeling rested and fit and he took off at a mile-eating trot. I was wearing my moccasins and every little while I'd dismount and run alongside of him. With that kind of relief a horse can go a long way without any substantial rest. Once we came to a stage station that was dark, but there was a watering trough out in front and we stopped for a drink and a short breather.

A full moon made the going easy most of the night. The sun was up when I spotted the stage station I was looking for silhouetted low and black against the southeastern sky. Smoke was rising from a stovepipe alongside the low adobe structure and I imagined I could smell the coffee boiling on the stove.

I had dismounted and was tying Old Dobbin to the hitching rail when the door of the building opened and a squat, unshaven man appeared in the doorway, a shotgun cradled in the crook of his right arm. He wore a surly look and a dirty shirt which was tucked haphazardly into the top of his jeans.

"Lookin' fer somethin', stranger?" he asked, an unfriendly undertone to his voice.

"Been ridin' most of the night," I said. "I could use me a cup of coffee."

"C'mon in," he said, standing to one side.

I followed inside and slumped at a long table that taken up the center of the room. He handed me a mug of new-made coffee. It was black and hot and it tasted good.

"Ridin' all night," he repeated. "You must be in a hurry to get somewhere."

"I've arrove," I said.

He looked at me in astonishment. "You've what?"

"I've arrove," I said. "This is where I was headed."

"Mind tellin' me why? Ain't nuthin' around for 30 miles in any direction 'ceptin' sagebrush and rattlesnakes."

"There's you, my friend," I said. "I come to see you."

He looked at me suspiciously. "Mister, I ain't never seen you in my life. You got me mixed up with someone else."

"Yer right," I said. "I ain't never seen you before, neither. I don't know yer name or anything about ya 'ceptin' you run this here stage station."

He scratched his head. "Ya got me beat. What the hell is it ya want?"

"Morgan Adams," I said.

He paled just a bit and looked away. "Who?" he asked. "I don't know no Morgan Adams."

"I think ya do," I said patiently. "Stocky feller. About forty. Wearin' a business suit. Was on the last stage that come through here. He got off, but he never got back on."

"Oh, that feller," he said, still not looking at me. "Told me he was in a hurry to get to Wichita Falls. So I sold him a horse and a saddle. He left before the stage pulled out. Ain't seen him since."

"I think yer lyin'," I said.

He turned and glared at me. "You callin' me a liar?" He began edging toward the shotgun which he'd leaned against the wall by the door.

I hauled out my six-gun. "Stay where ya are," I said. "I need some answers before I kill ya."

He turned a couple of notches paler. "Looky here, Mister. I don't know what yer talkin' about. Like I told you the feller bought a horse and took off."

I stood up suddenly, stepped over to him, and backhanded him across the face.

He staggered backwards, shook his head a time or two, and started to charge me, but the sight of the gun brought him up short. He glared at me and wiped a dirty sleeve across bloody lips.

"There wasn't no call for that," he mumbled. "I tole you the truth."

I aimed my gun carefully at the toe of his boot and pulled the trigger. The sound of the shot echoed loud in the closed room, but not loud enough to drown out his scream. He sat, almost fell, on the floor and pulled off his boot. He wasn't wearing socks and there was a lot of blood where his middle toe had been.

"Oh God," he whimpered over and over. "Oh God. Oh God."

"God or nobody else ain't gonna help you less'n you tell me what happened to Morgan Adams," I snarled. "After I've shot off yer toes I'm gonna go to work on yer fingers."

"He's buried out in back," he whispered, rocking back and forth in pain and shock. "But I didn't kill him. Honest to God I didn't."

I walked over to the counter, picked up a dirty towel, and threw it at him. "Here. That'll help stop the bleedin'. Now tell me what happened 'cause I'm tired of foolin with ya."

"That old lady who come in on the stage with him. She done it. Got him to go out in back with her and stabbed him with a hat pin. Ya wouldn't think that'd kill anyone but she had some kind of poison on it. Paid me $10 to bury him and told me to keep my mouth shut or I'd get what he got. I don't want nuthin' to do with that old woman."

"Mister," I said, "you bandage up that toe good an' tight 'cause you and I are heading out of here for Wichita Falls. There's a doctor there can fix you up right and a sheriff who'll wanna ask you some questions and when he does yer answers to him better be the same as they was to me."

Whilst he was fixing up his foot I found some bacon that I fried along with some bread that I soaked in the bacon grease and fried also. I offered some to him but he wasn't hungry. When I'd had another cup of coffee I marched him outside, if you could call his hippity-hop marching, saddled us up each a fresh horse, put a lead rope on Old Dobbin, and taken off for Wichita Falls.

It was late when we got there and I was bone tired. The sheriff had gone home for supper but there was a gnarled old man sitting at his desk with a deputy's badge on. I turned my prisoner over to him and after he was safely in a cell I headed back to the hotel. In three nights I had yet to sleep in the room I'd rented but I figured three was a charm so I'd try again. I went up the stairs and down the hall, pausing again at the room where Liddy Dole and the old woman were staying, but all was quiet there.

In my room I tugged off my boots and lay back on the bed after carefully checking around for another one of the deadly corks. By the time I was stretched out flat I was fast asleep and stayed that way until midmorning when a hard knock on the door aroused me.

CHAPTER 11

IT SEEMED LIKE for the last week or so whenever I got a chance to get a good sleep someone came along and woke me up. Only time it didn't make me mad was that time at Ada's house.

"Hang on. I'm comin'," I hollered, swinging out of bed and reaching for my pants.

I was still buckling my belt when I opened the door. It was Sheriff Smith.

"Told ya I'd be back, Sheriff," I grinned.

He didn't smile back. "Feller ya brought in last night is dead," he said. "Kilt."

"Dang," I said fervently, then added, "It weren't me, Sheriff. I fell in bed last night and never heard a thing until you knocked."

"Ain't blamin' you," he said, "but thought you might like to know. I think he was poisoned."

"You sure?" I asked. "Him, too?"

"What d'ya mean, 'Him, too?' "

"He told me that old woman with Liddy Doyle poisoned Morgan Adams at his stage station. Then paid him to bury him. That's why I brought him in. Thought you'd wanna talk to him yerself."

"Well, I'll be damned," he swore. "Naw, I ain't sure he was poisoned. But it seems likely. He was dead in his cell this mornin', face all contorted up. Don't seem likely it was a heart attack or a stroke. Deputy said he was fine last night when he turned in. Foot was hurtin' though. Deputy said he complained that you shot off his toe."

"Gun went off by accident, Sheriff," I lied, smiling just a bit. "Promised him I'd get him a doctor this mornin'. Ya don't suppose he bled to death, do ya?"

He ignored me and said, "Look, whyn't you get dressed and meet me downstairs in half an hour? We'll have some coffee and talk."

I joined him in half the time and we went into the restaurant where we both had coffee and I had two slices of ham, six eggs and a platterful of fried potatoes. Best meal I'd had in days, but nothing tastes as good in the morning as coffee and that was good coffee, not a bit of chicory in it.

By the time I'd finished eating we'd been joined by the town marshal whose name, it turned out, was also Smith.

"Hasn't always been," he admitted, "but when I was younger and dumber I got in a little trouble, nuthin' serious, but when I straightened out I figured a new start meant a new name. Smith here"—he indicated the sheriff—"is the only born Smith I ever knew."

"I asked the marshal to join us," Sheriff Smith said. "We work good together and we keep each other abreast of what each of us is doin'."

"I been thinkin'," I said. "If that feller was poisoned that old lady had to do it, but how?"

"That cell is ground level," the sheriff said. "If she knowed he was there, might be she could get at him from the outside. Far as that goes, if the deputy left for a few minutes she could get at him from the inside. Be risky but it could be done. Come to think of it, he wasn't on his cot; he was lyin' close to the front of the cell when the deputy found him this mornin'. Might be she did get at him from the inside. I'll have to find out if the deputy left for any reason."

"In the meantime one of you ought to make sure that old woman don't leave town," I suggested.

"Already thought about it," Marshal Smith said. "I checked the register and she's still in the hotel. Train don't come in until tomorrow and the feller at the stage station has been told to let one of us know if she tries to buy a ticket."

"Why don't ya just arrest her?"

"Fer what? On yer say-so that a dead man said she killed Morgan Adams? 'Less we can find someone who saw her go into the jail last night we ain't got proof that she's done anything, and even if someone saw her go in we still don't know she poisoned him. No, we'll just keep an eye on her fer now."

"Can't ya at least get Liddy away from her?"

"Not unless she wants to leave. All we got so far is yer story that she don't want nuthin' to do with you. One look at you, though, and it's easy to see why."

Both the Smith boys chuckled and I couldn't blame them. It wasn't enough that I needed a shave and a haircut. Even with both I wouldn't have been no raving beauty, with that white blaze across the side of my skull where a bullet had cut a deep furrow and that knife scar on my left cheek where a quick and dangerous Mexican in El Paso had caught me zigging when I should have been zagging.

I shrugged. "She don't mean nothin' to me, only her pa was a saddle pardner of mine and I figure I owe her."

I swallowed the last of my third cup of coffee and got up. "You gonna want me for anything, Sheriff?"

He shook his head. "See ya around," he said.

I went on down to the stable to check on Old Dobbin and the roan. I took a few minutes to curry them and gave them both a bait of oats. On the way back I thought I caught a glimpse of the old woman turning into the general store. As I went by I looked in to be sure it was her. It was and she was alone. On impulse I headed

121

for the hotel at a run. Striding through the lobby I took the stairs two at a time. Stoppin' in front of Liddy's door I knocked loudly. There was no answer.

"Liddy," I called softly.

There was no reply but I thought I heard a noise on the other side of the door. I tried the knob. The door, not surprisingly, was locked. To hell with this, I thought. I took a step back and hit it with my shoulder. It was a flimsy door and it flew open.

The curtains were drawn and the room was semidark. Then I saw her. She was lying on the bed on her back. Her hands were tied together and tied to a bedpost. The same thing had been done to her feet. She was gagged. She stared at me with wide, wild eyes. I took my Barlow folding knife from my pocket and quickly cut the light ropes that bound her. A second later I had removed the gag.

"Oh Del. Thank God, thank God," was all she could say.

"Can you walk?" I asked.

She nodded and stood up.

"Come with me. Now!" I ordered. Taking her hand I pulled her down the hall to my room.

"You wait here," I said. "And don't say nothing or answer the door unless you recognize my voice. Hear?"

She nodded again. I went over to my saddlebags and dug out a small twin-barrelled derringer I had taken away from a cheating gambler one night in Mobeetie.

"That woman comes here you'll know I'm dead," I said. "So you shoot her. Don't ask no questions, just shoot her."

She nodded her understanding and I went out, closing the door behind me. I waited a second until I heard the lock click.

Going back to Liddy's room I went in and closed the door behind me. I had busted the jamb on the inside but from the outside everything looked normal. I moved the only chair in the room to one side and sat down with my gun in my lap. It was only a few minutes before I heard the old woman pause outside the door.

In a moment she entered, saying, "I'm back, dearie. Have you been good?"

"Sure enough," I said from the side of the room where I was sitting.

She gasped, but quickly regained her composure.

"How dare you break in my room like this," she said indignantly. "I've a mind to call for help."

As she talked she moved slowly toward me.

"Holler if ya want," I said, "but you take one more step, auntie, and yer dead meat." I lifted my gun so she could see it was pointing directly at her.

She stopped in her tracks. "Now," I said, "set yer bag on the floor very carefully, then go over and sit on the bed."

"Now then, old woman," I said, "start tellin' me what this is all about."

"I don't know what you're talking about," she snapped.

"Liddy Doyle says ya do."

"Go to hell, cowboy. You can't prove anything and neither can she."

"Fair enough," I said. "But I'm gonna let you tell yer story to the sheriff and the marshal. I don't believe ya, but maybe they will."

She was hard as nails. "Suit yourself," she said indifferently.

I stood up and waved my gun at her. "On yer feet, lady," I ordered. "Now you walk out in front of me."

She headed for the door with me moving right behind her. It was nearly the last thing I ever did.

She raised her right hand casually to her hair, which was piled high on her head. Then, unexpectedly, she dropped it down, at the same time swinging swiftly around and stabbing out at my face with a long pin she had pulled from her hair. In the nick of time I saw it coming and leaped back, at the same time slashing the barrel of my gun across her wrist. I heard the bones crack and she screamed in pain and dropped the pin. Cradling her right arm against her breast with her left hand she sank moaning to the floor. Without taking my eyes or my gun off of her I reached down and carefully picked up the pin by its blunt end and stepped back.

"You broke my wrist," she whimpered.

"Get on yer feet right now before I kick ya onto 'em," I snarled. "You try somethin' funny again and we'll see how you like bein' stuck with yer own pin."

Instinctively she shrank back and then climbed slowly and painfully to her feet.

"Now move," I said.

With her walking ahead of me, I holstered my gun and we went down the stairs and through the hotel lobby with nobody looking at us twice. "Don't even try to run," I whispered to her, "or you'll have a busted leg to go with your busted arm."

She didn't answer and we went out the door and down the board sidewalk to the sheriff's office. He was in.

"I got a present for ya, Sheriff," I said. "This here is the lady who I think killed Morgan Adams and probably killed that feller I brought in last night. She was holdin' Liddy Doyle captive. I found her tied and gagged.

"When this sweet thing come back to the room she tried to stab me with this here hat pin. That's how she got her wrist broke.

"Sheriff, I'm willin' to bet my eyeteeth there's poison on this pin."

"Don't be ridiculous," she said. "Sheriff, this man broke into my room and assaulted me. I want him arrested.

"And I want a doctor because the sonofabitch broke my arm," she added venomously.

"Ha!" I snorted. "You got the wrong Smith. That little trick worked for Ada Venn with the marshal but it ain't gonna work here."

"Dang it, Tackett, don't be too sure," the sheriff said. "All I got is yer word against hers. How do I know she ain't tellin' the truth? How do I know that pin is poisoned? And where's that Doyle gal you keep talkin' about?"

"I can fetch Liddy Doyle," I said, "but you'll say the same thing—that it's her word against this lady's.

"But I tell ya what. Ask her to stand still whilst you jab her with this here pin, just enough to draw blood. And we'll see if it's poisoned or not."

The sheriff looked at her. "That all right with you, ma'am?"

"Oh," she suddenly moaned. "My arm. It's killing me. Get me a doctor."

She started to sink slowly to the floor. The sheriff reached out and caught her and eased her into a chair. She seemed to be in a faint. The sheriff asked me to fetch some water. Instead, I moved up beside him.

"I'll get the water in a second, Sheriff. First, though, I'm gonna jab her with this here pin."

Immediately she sat erect. "You sonofabitch, don't you touch me with that," she snarled.

I looked at the sheriff. "It's up to you," I said.

"Go ahead," he said. "It won't hurt much, ma'am, and it'll help prove yer innocence."

I leaned forward bringing the point of the needle close to the back of her hand.

"No!" she screamed. "No! No! It's poisoned."

I stood up. "Satisfied, Sheriff?"

"Yeah," he said, "but that still don't prove she killed Adams or this other feller."

"Ask her," I suggested, thrusting the pin close to her hand again.

"All right, all right," she blurted. "I killed them, but you can't prove it and I'll deny it in court."

"Maybe, maybe not," the sheriff said. "Right now I'm takin' you to the doctor to fix that arm, then I'm holdin' you on a charge of kidnappin'.

"Tackett, you go find that Doyle gal and bring her in here to sign a complaint, hear?"

"By the way," he asked. "How'd she break her arm?"

"She tried to stab me with that pin and accidently banged it against the barrel of my gun," I said.

"You have a lot of accidents with that gun," he said sarcastically.

He went out, leading the old woman toward the doctor's office. Me, I headed back to the hotel. When I reached my room I knocked and called, "It's me, Del."

In a moment she'd opened the door and flung herself into my arms. Her body was wracked with sobs and I held her tight against my chest, stroking her hair with one hand. After a few minutes she pulled herself together and looked up at me with red eyes, a runny nose, and a tear-stained face. I went over to the bed and ripped off a corner of the well-worn sheet.

"Here's a hanky," I said.

She took it and blew her nose and wiped her eyes.

"Ya wanna tell me what happened?" I asked, as she sat down on the edge of the bed.

"It was terrible, Del. It was just awful. That old lady—she's not really all that old, she's just made up to look old—she, she killed poor Morgan Adams—at least she said she did—and told me she'd kill me if I didn't do exactly what she said. She threatened to stab me with a hat pin that she said had some kind of deadly poison on it. Ohhhh."

Sobbing, she buried her face in her hands for a moment while she regained her composure. Then she looked at me pleadingly. "Did she kill Morgan Adams? He was such a nice man."

"Looks as if," I said. "Go on, what happened next?"

"You know the rest. She brought me here and said we had to stay here until she heard from the man she's working for."

"She say who he is?"

"No. But she's waiting for a wire from Denver."

"Could be Crispen Giucy. That was where he was headin'," I said. "When was she expectin' the wire?"

"Tomorrow, I think she said."

"Did she go out anytime last night?" I asked.

"Yes, she did. She was angry. She was looking out the window and suddenly started cursing. She did that a lot when no one else was around. Then in a little while she said she had to go out and take care of someone."

"Someone or some thing?"

"Someone, she said. Then she tied me to the bed the same way you found me today and went out. She was gone about half an hour. The only thing she said when she came back was, 'That solves one problem.'"

"It did," I said. "She sneaked into the jail and killed the feller she'd paid to bury Adams. I brang him in to tell the sheriff what he knew but he never got a chance to talk."

"What will we do now?" she asked.

"First thing we got to do is go down and let you sign a complaint against her. Then when the train for Denver comes in tomorrow we'll climb aboard and go see what we can do to get what you got comin' to you."

A sudden thought struck me.

"Someone killed Ada," I said. "Choked her and threw her off the train to Denver."

Liddy turned pale. "How terrible," she gasped. "I know she was trying to steal from me, but we had been friends and she'd been good to me. Oh, this is just awful.

"And all because Daddy grubstaked that man who found the

mine. It's not worth going to Denver if more people are going to be killed."

I spoke harshly. "Don't be silly. It's yers and we're goin' to go get it. You can't blame yerself if people get greedy. After what you been through it's more important than ever that you get what's yers. Now, come on. We got to go see the sheriff."

CHAPTER 12

FOUR DAYS LATER Liddy and I got off the train in Denver. It was already a good-sized city, thanks to the mining boom that had been going on in Colorado for the last fifteen years. Liddy had pretty well recovered from her ordeal at the hands of the old lady, except that she wasn't all that old, after all.

It turned out she had made herself up to look twenty years older than she was, which was no more than forty. She wasn't talking to the sheriff or anyone else, although she'd summoned one of the two lawyers in town to represent her. Letters in her handbag identified her as Mrs. Dorothy "Dot" Matricks from Kansas City. One of the letters was from a city councilman in Abilene named Crispen Giucy who had noncommittally asked her to come to Abilene because he had a job for her. He had promised that it would be "well worth your while," but he didn't go into any detail.

Liddy had signed legal papers accusing Dot Matricks of kidnapping her and holding her by force and threat of force against her will.

The justice of the peace in Wichita Falls had refused to let her out on bail and it would be two weeks before a circuit judge was due in the town. At that time he would set a trial date and the sheriff would wire Liddy in Denver to tell her when she had to return to testify. In the meantime, she was free to travel so long as she kept Sheriff Smith informed of her whereabouts.

Liddy and me checked into separate rooms at the new Palace

Hotel where we'd wired ahead for reservations. The desk clerk greeted me effusively as Mr. Sackett.

"Yours is a prominent name in Colorado," he gushed.

"No it ain't," I said. "The name is Tackett."

His face fell, but then he brightened. "I have a lovely suite for you and Mrs. Tackett."

It fell again when I told him I wanted two singles, that "Miss Doyle and me ain't married nor are we likely to be."

That last remark didn't seem to make Liddy happy either but I laid the slight downturn of her mouth to her being tired from the long train trip.

We'd arrived in midmorning and since the arm in which she'd been shot was still bothering her some, I told her to rest up until noon. Then we'd have some lunch and afterward we'd look up Kooby Rarbil's law firm and find out what that situation was.

Denver was a busy, bustling town with new buildings going up everywhere, some of them several stories high. Colorado was already a state, having been admitted to the Union in 1876 with Denver as its capital.

After we ate, the hotel clerk was able to give us directions to the law firm of Rarbil, Tomes and Emulov and we walked the three blocks or so to its offices. She didn't have much to say as we walked so I let my mind drift back over the past few days.

The trip from Wichita Falls to Denver taken nearly three days and during that time we'd talked about a lot of things: About her father, old Billy Bob Doyle, a former ranger who'd lost an arm as the result of a bullet wound and later been cut down by a man he'd taken to be a friend. He was the reason I had gone to Abilene and he was the reason I was trying my best to see that nobody stole her inheritance from her.

And I'd told her again, this time in more detail, about Ma's diary and how I was anxious to learn to read so that I would know what was in it.

"I don't rightly know who I am," I told her, "or where we come from. My earliest memories are of Carson City and leavin' there in the dark of night after Ma killed a feller who was trying to attack her. He had powerful friends, so Ma packed up a burro and we walked with it all the way to the Sierra goldfields.

"I growed up there but Ma never talked about what lay behind us. Maybe it was because she was too busy tryin' to pan enough gold out of them mountain streams to keep body and soul together. Never had no time either to teach me to read or write. I didn't have no schoolin' at all.

"When I was sixteen she told me it was time I went out on my own. I had saved enough money doin' odd jobs around the camp to buy a beat-up old saddle and a crowbait of a horse, so I saddled up and drifted. Never went back neither, until word reached me in Salt Lake that Ma had died. I went back then to make sure she was buried proper. Turned out the only thing she left behind was this diary and I got to know what she wrote in it."

Liddy was very kind. "I'd be glad to read it to you and I would never breathe a word of what's in it to anyone."

"I can't let you do it, Liddy," I said. "I just got me a strong feelin' that I don't want to share what's in it with nobody. I'd hoped that maybe when I come to Abilene I could pay ya to teach me to read. I got a little money saved up, but shucks, yer gonna be a rich young lady pretty quick and'll have better things to do."

"Don't be silly, Del," she retorted. "After all you've done for me I would love to teach you to read. As a matter of fact, we could begin right here on the train."

She reached in her bag and brought out a well-worn book that turned out to be Dickens' *A Tale of Two Cities*. She explained that it had been her mother's favorite book and was also hers.

"We won't start reading it right away," she said. "First I want you to learn the basics. The alphabet and the sounds of the letters. You know, there are only forty or so sounds in the English language and if you know what letters make those sounds you will be able to read. When I teach reading at school I use a system called phonics which means that I have the children sound out the letters in a word. It's easy and almost every child can learn to read that way. So certainly you can too. Shall we begin?"

She looked at me expectantly. But suddenly a great wave of shame at my ignorance flooded over me.

"I think I'd rather wait until we get your situation taken care of," I said, not looking at her.

"Why, Del," she said, taking my hand. "You're afraid. And there's no need to be. If you want me to teach you to read, we're going to start right now. Otherwise you'll just have to find some-one else."

She reached in her bag again and fetched out a notepad and a pencil. On the pad she wrote the alphabet in capital letters both as they are printed and as they are written.

"I want to teach you to write, too," she said. "But the reading comes first."

She started out by having me memorize the alphabet and by explaining the sounds the letters and combinations of letters made and we went from there. It wasn't as hard as I thought it would be and I found that over the years of my drifting I had learned more than I knew I had. One of my problems had been that I didn't think I could read so I didn't try. Now I was trying and by the time we reached Denver I could read, slow, I admit, but I could read whole sentences from that Dickens book. When I'd come to a word that was strange, she'd say, "Sound it out," and I found out I could.

"But this is printin'," I said. "And Ma's diary is in handwritin'."

"That's the easy part," she assured me. "All you have to do is recognize the alphabet as it is written rather than as it is printed. Here, let me show you."

But by then we had reached Denver and that part of my schooling had to wait, because here we were, walking to the law offices of Kooby Rarbil and the task in front of us was to secure her inheritance. After that, she or somebody would have to take me the next step and teach me how to read writing. But for the first time in my life I had a little confidence in my mind and in my ability to learn something besides riding a horse or shooting a gun. And that was worth a whole lot.

We were quiet as we walked, but I was happier than I could ever remember being, and more sure of myself.

Kooby Rarbil's law office was on the third floor of a new four-story building that had both stairs and a newfangled thing called an elevator. An old man operated it and would take you to any floor you wanted to go to. You, maybe, but not me. Liddy stepped right on aboard and tugged at my arm, but I pulled back. "I'll walk up," I said. "See ya there."

"You're afraid," she teased.

I thought it over for a brief moment, then nodded. "Guess yer right," I said. "See ya there."

She was waiting for me outside Rarbil's office. We went on in and a well-endowed young lady seated at a desk looked us over coolly.

"We wish to see Mr. Rarbil," Liddy said. "I am Elizabeth Doyle. I have corresponded with him and I believe he is expecting me."

"I'm sorry, but Mr. Rarbil is out of the city," the young lady said, not looking a bit sorry but eyeing me appraisingly.

"Oh, dear," Liddy said in disappointment. "I have come all the way from Abilene, Texas, to see him."

"One of his partners, Mr. Tomes, is in," the receptionist said, not taking her eyes off of me. "Perhaps he'll see you."

She stood up, making sure I got a good look at her figure, which was one of those hourglass shapes and well worth looking at. I followed her with my eyes down a hallway until she came to a door, knocked, and disappeared inside.

Disappointed as she was, Liddy hadn't missed that little bit of byplay. "Pretty girl, isn't she?"

"I hadn't noticed," I said.

"We must visit an eye doctor while we're in Denver," she said, amusement in her voice.

Before I could think up a suitable answer the girl came out of the office and walked down the hall toward us and I was able to notice that she looked as good coming as she did going.

"Mr. Tomes will see you," she said. "His is the first office on the right."

"Come, Del," Liddy said, taking my arm and tugging me along.

LeVon Tomes was a strikingly handsome man, tall and slender with features you'd expect to see on one of those Greek statues you find in a museum. But he wasn't Greek; he was clearly a Negro.

I must have been staring because he smiled at me, showing even white teeth. "You look surprised. I don't blame you. Most folks don't expect to see a lawyer who is a Negro."

"Friend," I said, "yer color don't make no difference to me. Man does his job, that's all I care about."

He smiled again and extended a large, well-manicured hand. "I'm LeVon Tomes. I'm a partner here with Mr. Rarbil and Mr. Emulov. I understand you are looking for Mr. Rarbil. I'm sorry but he has been called out of town on client business."

He had a firm grip and he looked me right in the eye as we shaken hands.

"This here is Miss Doyle," I said.

"I'm pleased to meet you," Tomes said. "How can I help you?"

He indicated chairs and we sat down. He pulled his chair from around his desk and joined us.

"My name is Elizabeth Doyle," Liddy said. "My father was William Robert Doyle, although people called him Billy Bob. He was killed several months ago in the Arizona Territory."

"I'm sorry," Tomes murmured.

Liddy blinked a couple of times, squeezing back a tear, and continued: "Papers he left, including two letters from Mr. Rarbil, indicate that he was in partnership in a silver mine with a gentleman named Oscar Taime, who, I believe, is also recently deceased."

Tomes interrupted. "Would that be The Wait and See mine in Bonanza?"

Liddy brightened. "Why, yes. Do you know it?"

The lawyer frowned. "Miss, may I see some identification?"

"You got problems, Mr. Lawyerman?" I broke in.

He looked me straight in the eye. "And what is your role in this Mister—er—Sackett?"

"The name is Tackett," I said. "Remember it. Miss Doyle's daddy was a friend of mine. I come along to make sure she got her rightful inheritance."

Tomes turned back to Liddy. "You do have some sort of identification, Miss—er—Doyle?"

"Doyle," I said. "There ain't no 'ers' in there."

Tomes didn't answer me. "Miss Doyle," he said. "I apologize. I didn't mean to question your identity but we have a difficult situation here."

Liddy had been fishing around in her handbag. "I have a few things here."

She handed him some papers to look at. He looked them over carefully.

"From these it appears that you are who you say you are. But it would help if you could show me the papers Mr. Rarbil sent to your father.

"Understand, Miss Doyle, I know quite a bit about this case. Mr. Rarbil and I have talked about it at length.

"As you must know, Mr. Rarbil located Mr. Taimes' only heir, a distant cousin from the same town you are from—Abilene. He is a Mr. Giucy, Crispen Giucy. Perhaps you know him."

"Too well," Liddy murmured.

Tomes frowned again and continued. "Mr. Giucy arrived here a few days ago. He had the papers Mr. Rarbil had sent to your father, along with a letter Mr. Taimes had sent him. He also . . ."

"Those papers were stolen from me," Liddy interrupted. "He had no right to them."

Tomes continued as if he hadn't heard her. "He also had what purported to be a bill of sale from you indicating that you had sold him your half of the mine . . ."

"I never . . ." Liddy began but Tomes kept talking.

"And a letter authorizing him to transfer the money from the bank in Bonanza to the bank in Abilene. Mr. Rarbil and Mr. Giucy should be in Bonanza now making arrangements to ship the money to Abilene."

Dang, I thought to myself, there's always some crook out there ready to take advantage of some helpless woman.

I stood up. "C'mon, Liddy. It looks like we got a lot of work ahead of us if yer gonna get what's yers. I don't think we can look to this lawyer feller for much help."

Tomes literally jumped to his feet, his eyes flashing with anger.

"Mr. Sackett or Tackett or whatever you call yourself," he said in a voice trembling with indignation, "you haven't even tried to see if I would help. This is a reputable law firm and we're not going to be a part of any scheme to cheat Miss Doyle, if that's what someone is trying to do. And let me tell you something else, Tackett. You think because you carry a gun you can bully people and talk to them any way you want. Well, you take your gun off, Mister, and I'll take you out in the street and kick the hell out of you."

"Be my pleasure, Mr. Lawyerman," I said, reaching down to unbuckle my gun belt.

Suddenly Liddy jumped between us. "Stop it, both of you," she snapped. "You two are acting like a couple of schoolchildren. And I won't have it."

Tomes looked at us for a moment and then busted out laughing. In spite of myself I found myself joining in. I stuck out my hand and he taken it in his.

"Sorry, Mr. Lawyerman," I said. "We been goin' through some rough times the last couple of weeks and my temper's runnin' a little short."

"I'm sorry, too," he said. "And I apologize for having challenged you because I would have had an unfair advantage. You see, before I became convinced that the only way to get ahead in the world is to get an education, I was a prizefighter, Marquis of Queensbury rules. I fought at 180 pounds which is a little light for a heavyweight, but I did pretty well, thirty-seven fights and only two losses. The last one was for the heavyweight championship against Ruby Bob Fitzsimmons and he knocked me out in two rounds. We had to fight in Canada because it's not a good idea for a black man to fight a white man here in the States.

"I thought about staying in Canada but I'm an American, born of free parents in Boston, so I don't have any experience with slavery. I came West because people out here are more interested in how you perform than they are in the color of your skin."

"And I am a damn good lawyer," he added fiercely, then more gently, "and I think that is what you need."

He gestured at the chairs. "Sit down, won't you please? That was quite a speech, wasn't it? I don't know what got into me because I like to think of myself as the strong, silent type."

He smiled again, showing his even white teeth.

"We have a problem," he said, after we'd talked a while. "I need to get word to Kooby to see if we can stop the transfer of the money from Bonanza to Abilene and unfortunately there is no telegraph to Bonanza and of course, no railroad. And unfortunately, too, we don't have wings, or even winged horses like Pegasus."

"Wouldn't that be wonderful," Liddy said.

"I ain't got the faintest idea of what you two are talkin' about," I said grimly, "but I'll get the word to Mr. Rarbil if you can write it out. I got two fresh horses at the stable. I understand Bonanza's about seventy-five miles from here. I can be there tomorrow mornin' if I leave here pretty quick."

"Fine," he said. "I'll have the letter prepared and bring it to your hotel within the hour. That should give you plenty of time to get ready. I think it would be better if Miss Doyle stayed with me in case I have any more questions. I will bring her to the hotel with me."

"I got a question," I said. "How will they ship the money?"

"As I understand it," Tomes said, "the money is sitting there in gold coins. Means they'll have to ship it by stage or wagon to the railroad at Pueblo and then by rail to Abilene."

I whistled. "All that gold sittin' in a vault up there. How come nobody's tried to steal it?"

"The banker up there is a tough old coot. He handles a lot of gold and silver. And to make sure it's safe he has men on guard around the clock. And they all know how to use a gun.

"When he makes a shipment three men go with it. A time or two someone's thought to try holding them up. They're all dead or in prison."

I left Tomes' office, taking a long look at the receptionist on my way out. She smiled and batted her eyes at me. I grinned at her and headed for the stairs. I still wasn't ready to try that elevator contraption.

At the end of the hour I had the horses saddled and ready to go and hitched in front of the hotel. The hotel chef had fixed me a couple of beef sandwiches which I had stuffed in my saddlebags. Now I was waiting in the lobby for Liddy and LeVon Tomes.

When they came in I got a shock. Tomes had shed his business suit and was wearing black jeans, a dark red shirt, and a black, flat-brimmed hat. There was a gun on his left hip with the butt thrust forward for an across-the-body draw.

"I'll go change and pack while you men talk," Liddy said, hardly pausing as they came in the door.

Tomes slouched down in a chair close to mine.

"We talked," he said, "and we decided her best bet was for the three of us to go to Bonanza and try to get there in time to face down Mr. Giucy. My partner, Mr. Rarbil, isn't going to be happy about being taken in this way. I'm certain he'll bring charges. By the way I have a rig outside with my horse tied to the back in case of emergency. There's a stage station we can stop at overnight and we should get to Bonanza by late tomorrow night."

"Can you use that gun?" I asked.

"If I have to," he said. "And I have a rifle in the buggy."

"Might be better if I left now," I said. "Make sure Giucy stays in town 'til you get there."

Without waiting for an answer I rose and headed for the door. I wasn't sure a buggy could get there in a day and a half; I knew I could.

CHAPTER 13

MY WANDERINGS HAD never brought me to Colorado before and even though I kept Old Dobbin and the roan at a steady trot I taken time to look around me. My trail lay south and west into the high mountains along the Continental Divide. Bonanza lay in the mountains west of Pikes Peak and along a creek that fed into the Arkansas River another 20 miles to the south.

The trail was wide enough for the buggy Tomes would be driving, or a stage, but not much more. Here and there recent heavy rains had cut shallow gullies across it and on occasion rocks had rolled down from the hillside and come to rest on the road. There was room for a man on horseback to get by but Tomes would have to stop and roll them aside to make room for the buggy. It was clear no stage or wagon had come this way for several days and this meant that for him and Liddy it was going to be a long, rough trip. I was willing to bet they would have to spend two nights on the road.

For the first part of my ride the mountains lay to my right; early snow had whitened some of their peaks. Below that they were green from the juniper, pine, fir, and other trees that grew along their sides. To the east the vast plains that reached from the Rockies to the Mississippi stretched into the distance until they were lost in the haze and the curve of the earth.

But after awhile the trail cut into the mountains, rising slowly but steadily. The stage station was here at the mouth of the canyon and there was smoke rising from the chimney and horses in the corral. A woman was standing at the door gazing off in the distance as I rode by. I waved at her but kept on going. In another hour the trail had leveled off, but by this time the sun had dropped well behind the mountains and I was riding in deep shadow. As it began turning dark I found a spot off the trail where there was a small stream and a patch of grass. It was here I made camp.

I unsaddled Old Dobbin and with handfuls of grass rubbed down both him and the roan. Then I built me a small fire, just large enough to heat water for coffee. I was sitting there sipping it and waiting for the fire to die down when I caught the faint sound of hoofs coming down the trail from the direction of Denver. I picked up the pot and doused the fire, then went over and stood by the horses to keep them quiet.

There were two of them and I could catch snatches of talk through the thin mountain air. I heard one say, " . . .Tackett feller must be one tough hombre."

The other said, "A bullet in the right place'll stop anyone."

The first one said, "Giucy must want to . . ." and then faded out.

I sat there in the dark and ruminated a spell. The two horsemen were headed toward Bonanza and they were in a hurry or they wouldn't be riding at night. And I, apparently, was at least part of the reason for their trip. One of them had mentioned Giucy and the only conclusion I could reach was that they were working for him. If that was true then they'd be laying for me in Bonanza. And I'd be easy to spot, big as I am and with that knife scar on my cheek and the white blaze of hair along the side of my head.

I shrugged. Wasn't nothing I could do tonight. I spread out my groundsheet, unrolled my blankets, yanked off my boots, and turned in. I would, as some folks say, sleep on it. Tomorrow would be plenty of time to figure out my next step. But sleep didn't come right away. There were too many questions running around in my mind. Who had tipped off those men that I was on the road to

Bonanza? Who, as a matter of fact, knew that Liddy and I were in Denver? Was Tomes mixed up in this?

After all, I'd never met him until today. And if he was involved, was Liddy safe with him? Puzzling over these and other unanswerable questions I finally drifted off to sleep.

I was awake at the break of dawn when you could still see the last few bright stars, and fifteen minutes later I was in the saddle, munching on the last beef sandwich as I rode. I rode carefully, looking for signs of the riders who'd passed me the night before, not wanting to come on them unawares. I'm not much of a tracker but the tracks of two shod horses on a rain-washed road are pretty easy to follow. I'd gone about a mile when I saw where they'd turned off alongside a small creek that crossed the road.

I figured they'd been looking for a camping place. That's why I was surprised when I felt something burn high on my left shoulder and heard the reverberations of a rifle shot. Without thinking I jammed my spurs into Old Dobbin's flanks. Startled and indignant he took a great leap forward and lit out running. Off to the side I heard another shot but Old Dobbin's leap had caused a second miss and before whoever it was could get off a third shot I was around a bend in the road and out of sight.

I kept Old Dobbin and the roan running for a mile before I slowed down and came to a halt beside a clump of large boulders. I swung in behind them, dismounted, and tethered both horses. My shoulder was stinging like I'd been attacked by a swarm of hornets and I stopped to examine it. The bullet had burned me enough to draw blood but it was already clotting and I decided to let it alone, at least until I had time to tend to it properly. I found my way around the far side of the rocks where I could keep an eye on the road without being seen.

I was mad clean through. Mad at myself for being careless and madder at whoever it was who had been shooting at me. I thought about waiting for them and bracing them and then decided that was stupid. They knew the country and I didn't. For all I knew there was a parallel trail that would take them around me or let them come up on my blind side. I kicked myself mentally and headed back for the horses at a run. In a second I was in the saddle and we were off at a gallop that I soon slowed down to a mile-eating trot.

It was noon when I come up on another stage station. I was tying the horses at the hitch rail when I heard the sound of hoofs and the whoop of a driver as a stage came racing in from the other direction. The driver pulled the team up with a flourish and tossed the reins to a boy who had appeared from behind the barn. I watched as the passengers began to climb down from the stage.

The first man off was a burly miner with black hair and a beetling brow. Right behind him came a slight little man, dapperly dressed in a suit and tie. His sandy hair was neatly combed and he was carrying a satchel that looked like it was meant to carry nothing more than papers. He slipped as he stepped off the stage and fell heavily into the miner.

Before the little man could excuse himself the big miner whirled around and snarled, "Watch what yer doin'."

"I beg your pardon," the little man said. "It was an accident."

He was wasting his breath. The miner was spoiling for trouble.

"I ought to bust you one," he growled, grabbing the little man by the front of his shirt and drawing back a heavy fist.

It wasn't none of my business, but I always figured if a feller is going to start a fight he should ought to pick on someone his own size.

I was standing about ten feet away so he had no trouble hearing me when I said, "Leave him be."

"Stay out of this," the miner growled, looking around.

"Let him go," I said.

"Who says?" he demanded.

"Me and my friend here," I said patting the gun at my side.

He let go of the little man and turned on me. "Yer brave with that gun," he said. "Take it off and I'll whomp yuh."

Suddenly all my anger and frustration welled up in me. I unbuckled my gun belt and tossed it to one side. He charged me and as he came in I swang an overhand right at him. He blocked it with his left forearm and kept coming.

In close he wrapped his arms around me, lifted me off the ground and began squeezing. He was a big, powerful man with huge arms and I could feel the breath leaving my lungs as he squeezed. Desperately I lifted both legs up and raked my heavy spurs down the back of his thighs, ripping his pants and cutting into the tender flesh.

He screamed and dropped me. As I hit the ground I brought my right knee up into his groin. He grunted and bent over, grabbing at his belly. I swung my right again and clouted him alongside his ear. He fell over on his side and I reached down, grabbed him by his shirt front, and hoisted him to his feet. I was drawing back my fist to hit him again when suddenly my anger disappeared and instead of hitting him I pushed him away. He staggered a few steps and sat down hard.

I turned and was picking up my gun belt when I heard someone shout, "Look out!"

Instinctively I dropped to my knees. A boot hit my side but the miner had not tried to kick me; instead he had taken a flying leap at me and when I ducked he flew over my head, kicking me as he went by, and sprawled headfirst into the dirt. As he scrambled to his feet I hit him alongside the jaw. This time when he fell I watched for a moment but he didn't move.

I turned and picked up my gun belt and buckled it on. The passengers had all gathered around to watch the entertainment. Now they headed for the door of the station and I fell in behind them, rubbing my bruised knuckles as I went. The little man came up beside me.

"You saved me from a terrible beating. I'm most grateful," he said.

"Wasn't nothing," I said.

"Allow me to introduce myself. My name is Kooby Rarbil. I am a lawyer in Denver. If I can ever be of service please don't hesitate to call on me."

I stopped and stared. "Yer Kooby Rarbil?"

"Do I know you?" he asked.

"Mr. Rarbil," I said, "you and me got to talk a minute. You can eat later."

I took him by the elbow and dragged him over to a wooden bench that was sitting in the shade of the stone stage station. We sat down and he turned and looked at me.

"Well?"

Quickly I told him about Liddy and her daddy and about Crispen Giucy and Ada Venn. I told him how Liddy and LeVon Tomes were following behind me in a buggy and how I was headed for Bonanza to stop Giucy from stealing Liddy's money, as well as The Wait and See mine. Rarbil listened me out, frowning.

When I finished he said, "There are some things you need to know because the situation is not as it appeared to be when I wrote to Mr. Doyle some months ago. Some of it is better and some of it is worse.

"In the first place, the mine has petered out. Most of the miners, including that bruiser you just whipped, have left and the mine isn't doing well enough even to pay wages for those who have stayed.

"That means that the only real asset is the fifty thousand dollars Mr. Taime deposited as Mr. Doyle's share of the profits. Now, unfortunately, I have made a terrible mistake. I accepted Mr. Giucy at face value—after all he is a member of the Abilene town council—and after he showed me the papers that now seem to have been stolen from Miss Doyle, and a letter, obviously forged, that appeared to be from Miss Doyle granting Mr. Giucy power of attorney, I accompanied him to Bonanza to vouch for him with the man who owns the bank there. I know the banker well and Mr. Giucy felt it would be better if I spoke directly to him rather than just send a letter.

"I am a damn fool," he added bitterly. "What I did is unforgivable."

"He's got the money, then?" I asked, my heart sinking.

He smiled suddenly. "No," he said. "But no thanks to me. Old Chase Hattan, the banker, was down in Pueblo on business and isn't due back until tomorrow. I felt I could stay no longer so I wrote him a letter vouching for Mr. Giucy."

"Mr. Rarbil," I said, "you got to come back to Bonanza with me."

He nodded a bit ruefully. "I know it. Let me get my valise from the stage and we'll see if we can procure a horse and saddle from the station manager. And soon as we get a bite to eat we'll go back to Bonanza."

"I got a extra horse," I said. "We get a saddle here we'll be in good shape."

We walked over to the stage and I climbed on top and found his valise and handed it down to him. Then we went into the station and found places at the end of the big long dining table. At the other end the miner was eating slowly. He looked up when we sat down but then looked away.

"That's a mean man. I'll never be able to repay you for what you did," Rarbil said.

There were still some slabs of beef and bowls of beans on the table, so we dug in. When we finished I went to find the station agent. He had a beat-up old saddle that he was willing to sell for $10 but didn't complain when I offered him five.

We were starting for the barn to get it when two men pushed open the door and strode into the room. They were dressed like cowboys but the hardware they wore indicated they were something more. They each wore only one gun, but their holsters were tied down and the walnut grips were made for use, not for show. The taller one, a slim, wiry blond man with cold blue eyes and a scraggly yellow mustache saw me and nudged his companion. He was shorter than the other and clean-shaven, but looked enough like him to be his brother. He, too, looked at me appraisingly, but neither one of them said anything. Instead they went to the now empty table and sat down. The agent brought them clean plates and they set about feeding their faces.

Rarbil and me went on outside and headed for the barn.

"You know," Rarbil said as we walked, "when those two men came in they looked familiar and I just figured out why. They were in the office a couple of times before I left, talking to Annabelle Schmidt, the young lady at the front desk. In fact, the first time the tall one came in he was with Giucy."

"I remember Annabelle," I said appreciatively. Then I snapped my fingers. "What do you know about her?" I asked.

"Nothing much. She's only worked for us a few months."

"Don't really matter," I said. "But some things are beginning to make sense now. Couple of fellers passed me in the dark last night where I was camped and I heard 'em talkin'. I heard enough to know they was headin' for Bonanza on Giucy's orders. They was to lay for me there.

"Couldn't recognize 'em in the dark but this has to be them. How would they know about me or know I was headed for Bonanza unless that girl told 'em? Looks to me like she's in cahoots with Giucy. Maybe he paid her.

" 'Nother thing. Somebody took a shot at me this mornin' on the trail. Could of been one of them. They was ahead of me; then they come in here behind me. Makes sense."

Rarbil nodded. "Does to me, too. What do you intend to do?"

"Go on to Bonanza and try to stop Giucy. I won't worry about these fellers until I have to."

We found the saddle and took it around in front to saddle the roan. The stage was just leaving and the two blond riders were still inside. Rarbil opened his valise and took out a gun belt and a Colt six-shooter and buckled it around his slender waist.

He looked incongruous in his city suit with that gun belt wrapped around him and in spite of myself I chuckled. He looked up. "Something funny?"

"That gun don't go with them fancy clothes," I grinned.

He smiled back. "Don't let the clothes fool you. Before I decided I didn't want to be a cowboy all my life I punched cows, went on a couple of trail drives, and worked as a deputy sheriff. Matter of fact, LeVon Tomes and Booker Emulov, my two partners, are pretty good fighting men, too. We all worked with our hands before we decided there were better ways to earn a living, better ways to live."

"You ought to think about that yourself," he added. "A man should do more with his life than punch cows or just drift. I don't know how much education you have but you seem like a smart gent. Think about what I just said when you've got time."

By this time he had tied his valise and carrying case behind his saddle. We mounted and took off at a fast trot. Suddenly I pulled up Old Dobbin.

"What is it?" Rarbil asked, coming up beside me.

"Them two fellers back at the station. You don't suppose they're waitin' there for Liddy and Tomes to show up? If they knew I was on the road they know they are, too."

"Maybe I'd better go back," Rarbil said. "Go down the road aways and warn them."

I shook my head. "Better I go," I said. "First off, you got to get to Bonanza in time to keep Chase Hattan from turnin' loose of that money to Giucy. Besides, Liddy Doyle is my responsibility, not yours. And on top of all that, no matter how good you used to be with that gun you got to be a little rusty. I ain't."

"You're right," he agreed. "I'll see you in Bonanza."

He touched spurs lightly to the roan and went galloping off down the road. I wheeled Old Dobbin and cantered back to the stage station. Inside, the two blond gunmen were loafing at the table, playing what looked to be a two-handed game of poker with a greasy deck of cards. They looked up when I came in and both of them did a double take.

"Howdy, fellers," I said cheerfully. "You want a third? I'm feelin' lucky."

The shorter man gathered up the cards and set them to one side. The taller one got slowly to his feet and began moving away from the table.

"Hope yer a better shot with a pistol than ya are with a rifle," I said conversationally.

"What's that supposed to mean?" he demanded.

"Nuthin' much," I replied. "Only someone took a shot at me down the road this mornin'. I figured it might be you boys. If it wasn't, well I been wrong before and I'm willin' to apologize. If I ain't, I thought I might as well come back and give ya another chance."

"You boys want to do some fightin' go on outside," a voice from the kitchen door said.

I looked over and saw the station agent standing there with an old-fashioned, Colt four-shot revolving shotgun in his hands. "Any shootin' here I'll do," he said.

The tall gunman smiled thinly. "Another time, cowboy," he said. "Come on Eddie, let's get out of here."

I moved over and blocked the doorway. "You ain't going any-where," I said. "Not fer a while, yet."

I turned to the man with the shotgun. "Mister, there's a man and a woman due in here later this afternoon in a buggy. I wanna be sure they get here. You turn these boys loose and they might not make it. You'd stop a heap of trouble if you'd keep 'em here until my friends arrive."

The agent shrugged. "Ain't my problem. You all can stay or go as ya see fit. But if ya stay ya shuck yer guns."

"Let's go, fellers," I said, standing to one side. "You first."

The agent spoke again. "Don't matter who goes first. Anybody tries any funny stuff and I'll cut him in two. Now git! All of ya."

I stepped quickly out into the yard and turned to face them. "Well, fellers?"

The tall one said, "Later. Come on, Eddie. We'll see this feller in Bonanza."

They mounted up and headed down the road in the wake of Kooby Rarbil. But he had a good head start and a fresh horse and I wasn't concerned. I went back inside and spoke to the station agent.

"Any way those two could circle around and head back toward Denver without comin' by here?"

He shook his head. "Ain't no trail. They could do it, I guess, but it'd take 'em a while."

"Guess I'll risk it," I said. I went outside and sat down on the bench. I leaned back against the building, pulled my hat over my eyes, and went to sleep. I don't know how long I dozed but eventually the sound of hoofs aroused me and I was awake and standing up when LeVon Tomes and Liddy barrelled into the yard behind a brace of matching bays.

Tomes tossed me the reins and I hitched the horses to the rail while he helped Liddy down. The three of us went inside and sat down at the long table. The agent came out of the kitchen, taken a long look at Tomes, but didn't say anything.

"You got anything to eat for a couple of hungry people?" Tomes asked pleasantly.

Before the agent could say anything, I said, "These are the folks I been waitin' for. If you can feed 'em quick we'll be on our way."

He didn't say anything but went back in the kitchen and presently came out with more beans and beef and a pot of coffee.

While they ate I drank another mug of coffee and told them what had happened and what Kooby Rarbil had told me about the mine and the money. When I'd finished Liddy spoke in a small voice. "I don't care. We've had nothing but trouble ever since we found out about the money and the mine. I was perfectly happy teaching and I won't mind going back to it at all. Del, let's go home. Let's go back to Abilene."

"Hold on a minute," I said. "Ain't nothin' we can do about the mine but there's no way I'm gonna let Giucy steal yer money. Tomes, if she wants to go home you take her back to Denver and put her on a train. Me, I'm goin' to Bonanza."

"After all," I added, "I can't let Kooby take care of things all by hisself. Giucy's gonna have at least two men there, maybe more."

"If Kooby gets there in time old Chase Hattan won't turn the money over to Giucy," Tomes reminded.

I laughed without humor. "If you think Giucy's gonna let Liddy have that money without a fight you got another think comin'. If he don't try to rob the bank he'll try to steal the gold before Liddy can get it shipped back to Abilene. I know it bothers you, Liddy, but there's gonna be bloodshed before we're through with this. You can bet on it."

"I'm not the same person I was back in Abilene," Liddy said. "I think I understand these things a little better. And I have confidence in you, Del. You do whatever it is you have to do. Furthermore, if you're going on to Bonanza then I'm going, too. That is if Mr. Tomes will take me."

"We'll go together," I said, rising. "It'll be safer that way."

CHAPTER 14

IT WAS MIDAFTERNOON by now and Bonanza was still 30 miles away which meant that we would have to spend one more night on the trail. As we left the stage station I rode well ahead of the buggy, keeping an eye out for any sign that the two blond gunmen might have left the road. My fear was that they would double back and lay in wait for us. But there was no sign of them leaving the road and if they had had any such idea they'd either thought better of it or were waiting much closer to Bonanza.

We'd come what I estimated to be about half the distance to Bonanza when I spotted a good camping place, a small patch of grass up against a steep incline about a hundred yards off the road. I stopped and waited for the buggy. When it came up we unhitched the two horses and pulled it behind a clump of trees out of sight of the trail. Then we led the horses over to the patch of grass. I unsaddled Old Dobbin and rubbed all three of them down with handfuls of dried grass, then picketed them where the grazing was good.

There was a trickle of water seeping out of the base of the incline and disappearing into ground almost immediately. But I managed to get a couple of hatsful of water, enough to give the horses a drink.

In the meantime Tomes had built a small fire and he and Liddy were making coffee and getting together a meal. While they were doing this I gathered up some grass and made a bed off to one side for Liddy.

It was still light so I decided to try to find a way to the top of the incline and see if I could spot a camp fire or other sign of the two gunmen. Directly behind us the incline was too steep to climb, but as I skirted its base I spotted a faint trail likely made by deer that climbed at an angle along the slope. I changed into my moccasins for easy walking and took off along the trail. It switched back and forth several times always taking me a little farther away from the camp. It finally came out on a wide ledge perhaps 500 feet above where we were camped and about a quarter of a mile to the south toward Bonanza. The sun had already set behind the mountain, leaving our side of the mountain in shadow.

Far off to the south I detected faint plumes of smoke that I figured must come from chimneys in Bonanza. But closer in there was nothing, no camp fires, no indication of any other people in the area. Trees and underbrush hid any sign of our camp. I was turning to begin my descent when I was startled by the sound of a single shot. It came from the direction of the camp. After the echoes died away there was dead silence.

I went down that trail fast, slipping and sliding and holding onto trees in my haste to get to the bottom. About two-thirds of the way down I stopped and began moving carefully and quietly. I didn't know what or who was down there or who had fired that shot and I wasn't about to walk in there without knowing. I came down on the flatland about two hundred yards from camp and paused, listening for I didn't know what. But all was quiet.

It was dusk now, which allowed me to move a little more freely without fear of being detected, but it also meant I would have almost no chance of spotting who, if anyone, was lurking in the scattered trees and underbrush. Moving carefully so as not to step on any dead branches, I finally got to within 50 feet of the fire. There was no one in sight. In the small meadow I could see the silhouettes of the three horses. They were grazing peacefully, unaffected by the sound of the shot.

Hugging the base of the cliff I crawled to within 20 feet of the fire. Searching the open area around it carefully with my eyes I spotted what looked like the outline of a body sprawled on the ground on the other side of the fire. As I watched it moved and I heard a groan. I didn't move. I didn't know who the person was. I didn't know if it was a trap to bring me out into the open. I didn't know who might be waiting for me out there in the shadows.

Suddenly, to the south toward Bonanza I heard the sound of hoofs and listened as they grew fainter and faded into the distance. At the same time the figure on the ground groaned again and struggled to sit up.

I called out in a low voice, "Tomes?"

A voice came back: "Tackett? Yeah, it's me. I'm shot."

"Lie still," I called back. "I'll help ya soon as I'm sure there ain't no one around."

"They're gone," he said. "They got Liddy and took off."

Well, I risked it, sort of. I skirted the fire, moving along the cliff side and came up on the other side of him, all the time listening carefully. But there was nothing, just crickets chirping and the sound of birds nesting down, and nothing disturbing them.

By now Tomes was sitting up. I walked over to him and helped him over by the fire. By its light I could see where a bullet had grazed his skull, close enough to knock him out and cut his scalp, but it didn't look like it was too serious. I added some wood to the fire and put on some water to boil. Going over to his carpetbag I rummaged around and found a clean shirt which I tore into strips. I bathed his wound and wrapped his head until he looked like he was wearing one of those turban things them other Indians wear.

He grumbled a little bit about me tearing up his shirt, but it was his wound so I figured it was only right to use his shirt. Besides, I was willing to bet that he owned more shirts than I did.

He told me it was the two blond gunmen, Eddie and the tall one. Eddie stayed back in the bushes and covered them from there while the tall one just walked out of the dusk and told them to put their hands up. He asked where I was but all Tomes told them was I was out scouting around. He and Eddie debated about waiting for me and probably would have except that the tall one got too close and Tomes tried to jump him. Eddie shot him from the brush but it wasn't that that knocked him out. As he reeled back the tall one clipped him alongside the head with the barrel of his six-gun. Even then he wasn't clear out, just unable to move.

He heard the tall one say, "Tackett must of heard that. Let's take the girl and go. We can get him later."

"The sonofabitch kicked me for good measure as he left," Tomes said, "and told me, 'That'll take care of you, nigger.' I won't forget that."

"Them horses of yers up to travelin' tonight?" I asked. "You can bet there's gonna be all kinds of trouble tomorrow in Bonanza and you and me oughtta be there for our share."

"I'm all right. I can travel and so can the horses," Tomes said.

I hitched them to the rig, tied Old Dobbin behind it, stamped out the fire, and put away our gear. In 15 minutes we were on the road to Bonanza. There wasn't room for Tomes to lie down but he leaned back and slept most of the night away anyway. I kept the horses going at a steady pace, stopping every now and then to give them a breather.

Dawn hadn't yet broken when we rolled into the main street of Bonanza. There was a stable on the outskirts of town and we pulled in there. By now Tomes was awake and aside from a headache was feeling pretty good. He set about unhitching the bays whilst I rousted out the hostler who grouched and grumbled until I gave him 50 cents to shut him up. We stabled the horses, rubbed them down with handsful of hay, and fed them with more of the same. Then we headed up the dirt street to the two-story Bonanza Hotel.

Bonanza was an old town, but its mining boom had begun only

about four years back. The Wait and See and three other big mines were the main but not only reason for its existence. There were a number of one- and two-miner digs scattered about in the hills. To the south there were several cattle ranches and a couple of Mexican sheep ranches. These were the original reason for the town's existence. With the coming of the miners the hotel had been built, and now there was a block-long business section and beyond that a string of saloons, and in back of them, up against the mountains, was a series of cribs. On the other side of Main Street was a church and a school and the homes of the respectable element.

There had been talk of bringing in both the telegraph and a spur railroad track, but six months earlier the mines had begun petering out and, instead of continuing to grow, Bonanza was rapidly shrinking back to something close to its original size. Already some of the stores were boarded up or just deserted.

All this I learned in bits and pieces in talking at various times to Kooby Rarbil, Tomes, and two or three of the people I met later in Bonanza.

But right now none of this concerned me. I wanted about an hour's sleep, a decent breakfast, and a talk with Rarbil. Then we had to figure out what to do about finding Liddy.

A sleepy clerk at the hotel signed us up for rooms. I asked him if Rarbil was staying there. He said yes, he'd checked back in late yesterday. He told us his room number and I decided to let Tomes get some rest until we could find a doctor for him while I went to roust Rarbil and find out what was going on. Only trouble was, when I knocked on his door no one answered. After knocking several times I tried the door and to my surprise it opened. I went on in and it didn't take no genius to see the bed hadn't been slept in.

First thing I thought was that I was in the wrong room, but Rarbil's valise and carpetbag were both on the floor so it was pretty clear that something or someone had kept him from coming back.

Remembering Ma's admonition about cussing, I said a soft "dang" and went out, closing the door behind me. Right now I knew I wasn't going to get no sleep for the time being and decided instead to get a cup of coffee and do some thinking. Wasn't no sense in rushing off in all directions because I didn't have the vaguest idea of where to look. Besides, a mug of hot, black coffee is a mighty fine aid to good thinking.

There was a dining room off the lobby and though it was early it was open for business. Right then I remembered that I hadn't had dinner the night before so when the middle-aged waitress came to my table I ordered a pot of coffee and some ham and eggs, seeing as how she told me they had gotten in some fresh ones. That coffee was about as good as I'd ever had and after eating four fried eggs, two thick slices of ham, and a double side of fried potatoes I was ready to face the day.

First thing I decided to do was go see the banker, Chase Hattan, and find out if Liddy's $50,000 was still in his vault. It was too early for the bank to open so I figured to track him down at home.

I went and found the hotel clerk who was wide awake by now and asked him if he knew where Hattan lived.

"I hope to shout," he said. "He's got the biggest, fanciest house in Bonanza. Actually it ain't really in Bonanza, it's about half a mile up the mountain. You go left out of the hotel and down the street until you come to a road coming in from the right. Just follow it on up the hill. His house is the only one up there. It's sitting off the road a ways, off to the right."

I thanked him and slipped him a quarter and headed for the door. Not forgetting that I had enemies in town, I opened the door a little way and peeked out. Then I stepped back in a hurry. Eddie, the short, blond gunman, was riding down the street on a red, spotted Appaloosa horse. When I was sure he was well beyond the hotel I stepped out just in time to see him turning onto the road that led to Hattan's house.

I hurried down to the corner and standing next to the building I took a look up the hill. Sure enough, there was Eddie and the Appaloosa.

Now what in hell is he doing going up there, I wondered. Then it came to me. That coffee had stimulated my brain pretty good and I knew why he was going to Hattan's. If Giucy and his men had Hattan they could take him to the bank and make him open the safe. Afterward they could use him as a hostage.

I thought to roust out Tomes but decided that he might not be in condition to fight. Besides I didn't know how much time I had. I walked on past the hotel and down to the stable. I threw a coin to the stable attendant and saddled Old Dobbin and headed down the street at a fast trot. At Hattan's road I paused and looked up it. It was empty. I rode up it about half a mile and then off the road about fifty yards. Dismounting, I tied Old Dobbin to a tree. I'd left my moccasins at the hotel so I reached down and undid my spurs, not needing the noise they would make.

The mountain had kind of leveled off here, making a wide shelf that was heavily wooded. I couldn't see it but I knew Hattan's place wasn't too much farther up the hill. I moved as silently as a body can in boots, watching out for dead branches and anything else that might make a noise if I stepped on it. It was only a couple of minutes before I spotted a structure in a clearing through the trees. At the edge of the clearing I stopped to look. Hattan had built himself a big, two-story house, Eastern style, with a circular driveway coming off the road and up to a long, wide front porch. There at the hitching rail stood Eddie's Appaloosa.

Behind the house was a combination barn and stable. Staying well back in the woods I circled around until I was behind the barn. I sidled carefully up to the back wall and edged down to the corner on the upside of the barn. From there I could see the edge of the house whilst nobody in the house would be able to spot me. Halfway along the barn wall was a side door that opened at my tug.

I ducked inside and stepped quickly to one side to avoid being silhouetted against the light. I waited until my eyes became accustomed to the gloom. There were half a dozen stalls and there was a horse in each one.

Just inside the main double-door entrance I caught sight of a boot projecting from behind a stack of miscellaneous worn-out farm equipment. I went over and took a look, being careful to walk where I couldn't be seen from the house. The boot was being worn by a dead man, a Mexican who must have been a hired hand. He wasn't wearing a gun or a gun belt but that hadn't stopped someone from shooting him down in cold blood. I guessed he'd been dead since at least the evening before.

As I straightened up I heard the sound of spurs jingling and someone whistling between his teeth. Silently I stepped back into the deep shadows beside the door, drew my gun, and, scarcely breathing, waited.

The man—it was Eddie, the short gunman—stepped inside and stopped to let his eyes get accustomed to the dim light.

"There's a gun pointed right at yer belly," I said conversationally.

He stopped in his tracks and I could see him tense up. "Yer a dead man if you try it," I said.

He drew a deep breath and relaxed.

"Unbuckle yer gun belt and let it drop," I said, moving to where he could see me.

"You!" he spit out. "Damn! I knew I should of waited for you along the trail."

"Every trail can't be a happy one," I said, stepping up close to him. "Now you want to tell me what's goin' on or should I slug ya on the head and go find out fer myself?"

"Go to hell!"

Instead, I slugged him alongside the skull with the barrel of my gun. He fell like a lightning-hit fir tree. There was rope hanging from the wall of the barn and I used it to hog-tie him tight. Then I dragged him over next to the dead man and turned his head so that when he came to he'd be staring into the staring eyes of the corpse.

"Happy trails," I murmured and walked over to where, standing in the shadows, I could survey the back of the house. Whilst I was standing there a Mexican woman came out and looked around and then went back inside. I sprinted the 50 feet across the yard, stepped lightly onto the porch, pulled the door open, and went inside, gun drawn. She turned at the sound of my entry and put a hand over her mouth to stifle a scream.

"It's all right, Señora," I whispered. "I won't hurt you. I'm a friend of Señor Hattan."

"Madre de Dios," she said, crossing herself. "Señor, if you are hees amigo you mus' help heem."

"You got to help me first, Señora. Quick, tell me what's happened."

"Two of them—Señor Giucy and another man I do not know—came yesterday morning and waited for Señor Hattan to come from the church."

I hadn't even remembered that yesterday was Sunday. In the last few weeks I'd lost all track of what day it was. A twinge of regret went through me. I wasn't a religious man, but every now and then I'd gone to church. Once I'd heard a preacher quote a piece of scripture sayin' that "The heavens declare the glory of God." That had stuck with me, and in my wanderings through the open spaces and the mountains and canyons and forests of the West I thought from time to time that these magnificent lands also declared His glory. It would be a terrible thing if another part of His handiwork—man—ever destroyed what He had labored over the ages to build.

She continued, "When Señor Hattan arrived here at the casa they tied heem up and put heem in the bedroom upstairs. I heard

161

them talking. In a leetle while they will take heem to the bank with them and make heem give them the oro—the gold—that is there.

"And, Señor, they have two other preesoners also. Yesterday afternoon they captured a man who came to visit Señor Hattan. He has been here before to veesit. Hees name is Señor Rarbil. Thees morning very early two more men came weeth a girl who they had all tied up. Thee man who is thee jefe—thee boss—Señor Giucy, was very angry. He said they should have keeled her and hidden her body.

"Señor, I theenk they mean to keel all of them."

"Who's the dead man in the barn?" I asked.

She burst into tears. "He ees my husband. He sought to escape and one of thee men shot heem in thee back. He ran into thee barn and thee man went after him and I heard another shot. Then thee man came back and told Señor Giucy, 'He ees not going anywhere now.' "

Without warning the kitchen door swung open and the tall, blond gunman strode in muttering, "Where in the hell is that damned Eddie?"

Then he saw me and stopped in his tracks. I shoved the señora out of the way and just stood there, waiting.

"What have ya done with Eddie?" he asked.

"He's sleepin' off a rap on the skull."

"Well," he said casually, "I knew it would come down to this."

And he went for his gun. Which he shouldn't have did. He wasn't near fast enough. I shot him twice in the chest before he had his gun out. He staggered back and tried to lift it and finally triggered one useless shot into the floor. For good measure, I shot him again and he crumpled to the floor and never moved.

A voice I recognized as Giucy's shouted, "Hank, what the hell's going on in there?"

I didn't say nothing, just reloaded my gun and waited.

"Hank?" Giucy shouted again with a question in his voice.

Then I heard him saying something I couldn't make out to the fourth man the Mexican woman had mentioned and then all was silent. I went over and picked up the broom and standing well to one side gently pushed on the door to the next room. Immediately two shots came crashing through it. At least one of them was still there. Then it struck me. Probably only one of them was on the other side of that door and the other one would be coming around on the outside.

Without thinking I dropped to the floor. At the same time a gun boomed and a shot whistled over my head and clanged off of a pan hanging on the wall. I whipped around and fired blindly through the window but didn't hit anyone. I fired again and rushed over to the window in time to see a man disappear into the barn. I ducked to one side just as another shot came through the window from the barn.

Dang, I thought. He's gonna turn Eddie loose and there'll be three of 'em to deal with and here I am holed up in the kitchen with Liddy and Rarbil and that banker feller upstairs.

Everything was silent for at least half an hour and then I heard low voices in the other room. That told me there were at least two of them in the house again, which meant one, probably Eddie, was still in the barn. I went over to the kitchen window and carefully raised my hat above the sill. Right then there was a shot from the barn and a bullet came whistling into the room and buried itself in the opposite wall.

Almost immediately thereafter I thought I heard footsteps on the floor of the room above me. Using the broom handle I pushed on the door again and again there was a shot and a voice that was not Giucy's said, "Stay where ya are, Tackett, and ya won't get hurt."

I didn't say anything, but went over to the stove and poured me a mug of coffee from the pot that was sitting there. It was black and hot and it tasted good. The Mexican woman had moved a chair over in a corner out of harm's way and was sitting there weeping silently.

Suddenly, from the other room I heard a new voice say, "Damn you, Giucy. I'm not going anywhere with you until you turn those two loose upstairs."

"You're coming all right," Giucy said. "Otherwise I'll send Kimby up to kill them now. You'd like that, wouldn't you, Phil?"

The third man's voice replied, "Anything you say, boss. You want 'em killed I'll kill 'em. You want 'em turned loose I might kill the little guy anyway and keep the girl for awhile."

"You stay here and watch 'em, Phil, and keep Tackett in the kitchen. Mr. Hattan and I are going to make a withdrawal from his bank. Move, old man!"

A second later I heard the front door slam and a few minutes later I heard a rig and two horses leaving the barn. At the same time Eddie unleashed a volley from his vantage point to make sure I couldn't take a shot at Giucy from the kitchen window.

As the hoofbeats faded in the distance the gunman, Kimby, in the other room, said, "Hey, Tackett. That your girlfriend up there? Let me tell ya what I'm gonna do with her."

He spent the next two minutes spelling out in graphic detail what his plans were. When he finished he laughed and added, "Maybe I can keep you alive long enough to watch," and laughed again.

As he spoke I felt an anger rising in me like I'd never felt before. Oh, I'd been killing mad in the past but never like this. And I knew that whatever happened this day, I was going to kill Phil Kimby if I had to walk through hell and a hailstorm of bullets to do it.

I thought back and counted the bullets that had been fired into the kitchen from the other room. There was three and I presumed Kimby had fired all three. If he hadn't reloaded that left two or maybe three in his gun. The unanswered question was, did he have one gun or two? Well, I had to figure only one and I had to figure that he hadn't reloaded that one, otherwise what I was contemplating not only wouldn't work but also would leave me a corpse on the floor of Chase Hattan's fancy house.

I took the broom and moved the door again. Nothing happened. I moved it farther and there was another shot. Immediately I shot back. I heard Kimby curse and then he fired another shot. In a split second I burst through the door, running low and throwing myself to one side as soon as I got through the doorway. A bullet just grazed my cheek and then I was on the floor, rolling to a sitting position and firing at a figure outlined against the far window.

In my haste I fired too quick and missed. A gun, obviously empty, came hurling at me. I dodged and scrambled to my feet. There was the sound of breaking glass as Kimby leaped headfirst through the window. I ran over to it and looked out, ready to shoot, even if I had to shoot him in the back as he was running away. No way that man deserved to live.

I saw him stagger to his feet clutching at his throat from which blood was spurting. He took a few steps and then fell in a heap. I went over to the door and went out and turned him over. He was still alive and tried to say something but he was choking on his own blood and all that came out was a gurgle. It was plain what had happened. In his haste he hadn't used his arms to protect himself when he leaped through the window and a jagged edge of glass had torn his throat open. As I watched him he coughed once and died.

I was sorry to see him go; I would have rather killed him myself.

CHAPTER 15

THERE WAS STILL Eddie to think of, but the first thing I had to do
was free Kooby Rarbil and Liddy. I ran back into the house and
took the stairs three at a time. The first bedroom was empty, but
Liddy was in the second one, lying on the bed with her arms tied to
the bedposts. Her hair was all awry and she had a bruise on one
cheek, but she managed a wan smile when I came in.

"Where have you been?" she asked with just the trace of a
tremor in her voice.

Without answering I took my Barlow folding knife from my
pocket and quickly cut the ropes that bound her. She sat up and
began rubbing her wrists, then suddenly burst into tears. I sat on
the bed and put my arms around her for a moment, but then
remembered Kooby Rarbil had to be up here somewhere.

"Get ahold of yerself, honey," I said. "I got to go find Kooby."

She drew back. "I'll go with you," she sniffled.

I took her hand and we went down a short hall to the third
bedroom. Rarbil was there, bound to a straight chair and gagged.
One eye was swollen almost shut. He had lost his coat and his shirt
was torn. It was plain he'd been slapped around pretty good.

He grunted when he saw us and I could see the look of relief in
his good eye. Quickly I cut him loose.

"You two stay here," I said. "There's still one of them fellers
runnin' around out there."

As I hurried down the stairs I heard the sound of hoofs. I ran to the door in time to see Eddie on the red Appaloosa rounding the corner that led from the driveway to the road. I snapped a prayer shot at him but he never even ducked and the sound of the Appaloosa's galloping hoofs soon faded.

"You two come on down," I hollered up at Liddy and Rarbil.

The Mexican woman came hesitantly into the room. "Have they gone, Señor?"

"They've gone, Señora," I said.

I turned to Liddy and Rarbil. "Liddy, you stay here with the señora. Kooby, you and me got work to do. Get a horse saddled and I'll bring mine up. We got to get down there and try and stop Giucy and that Eddie feller."

I was headed into the woods to get Old Dobbin when in the distance I heard two pistol shots, one within a split second of the other. What the hell, I wondered. I had no idea what the shots meant or who was shooting. I found Old Dobbin and headed through the woods back to the house to wait for Rarbil.

I had just pulled up in the yard when a horse and rider who looked like he was wearing a white turban came racing up the driveway. It was LeVon Tomes, wearing a satisfied look on his face.

"I got Eddie," he said. "I'd rather have gotten the tall one, but that's one of them won't be calling anyone 'nigger' again."

"I got his friend," I said grimly, as Kooby rode around the side of the house. "Ain't no time to talk. We got to get down to the bank."

The three of us rode down to Bonanza, two who had decided to be something more than just drifters and me, a drifter still and maybe—and it scared me to think of it—a drifter always. But maybe not. Just in the last few days Liddy had taught me to read a little and that was a start. If Kooby Rarbil and LeVon Tomes could make something of themselves then there wasn't no reason why I couldn't do it, too. Not if I really wanted to.

We drew up in front of the Bonanza Bank and swung down from our horses. The sign, printed in gold on the big plate glass window, read Bonanza Bank, Chase Mann Hattan, president. I wondered idly if he was related to the fat bartender I had run into and decided he wasn't. I went up and tried the door. It was locked. A townswoman lingering nearby said, "It doesn't open until 10 o'clock, in about 15 minutes."

"You fellers wait here. Let me check around in back," I said.

I found an alleyway between the bank and the general store and made my way around to the back, gun drawn. There wasn't much back there, some discarded junk and a series of outhouses. There were enough new moons out there to inspire someone to write an operetta. The business buildings backed up on the backyards of some of the townspeople.

A couple of ten-year-olds were playing in one of the yards. When they saw me they came over. "Mister, are you going to rob that there bank?" the fat towhead asked.

"Not today," I said. "Tomorrow, maybe."

"Whatcha got your gun out for, then?"

"To shoot nosy little kids. Now beat it," I said.

They taken off running and when they got close to the house, the fat kid began hollering, "Ma! Ma! He's got a gun. He's gonna shoot us."

"Dang!" I said and went over and tried the back door to the bank.

I wasn't surprised when it opened to my tug. I stepped inside and closed the door behind me. I didn't want that fat kid's ma to come out looking for me and find the door open.

With the door closed it was dark, but before I shut it I saw that I was in a kind of storeroom with another door on the other side of the room. I felt my way to it, moving carefully because I didn't know who might be in the bank. When I reached the door I stood to one side and shoved it open. A shaft of light came in but there wasn't no sign of anybody. I peeked around the edge of the jamb and saw a hall ahead of me that seemed to open out into the bank proper. Halfway down the hall was a door with glass on the top half. The words Chase Mann Hattan, president, had been painted on it. I pushed it open and when I did I heard a grunting sound.

I leaped inside, pointing my gun every which way at no one. Then I seen them, the two guards Hattan had hired to watch Liddy's $50,000. They were on the floor, neatly hog-tied. One had a bloody scalp. The other one was doing the grunting.

I whipped out my knife and cut his arms free. "You take care of your pardner. I'll be back in a minute," I said.

I went out to the main room of the bank. The big walk-in safe behind the teller's cage was open. A man who I took to be Hattan was sprawled on the floor. He had a wicked knot on the back of his head but I could see that he was still breathing. I went over and went through his pockets until I found a key ring. In half a minute I was letting Rarbil and Tomes inside and locking the door behind them, keeping out the woman who'd been waiting for the bank to open. In a minute, however, the door was unlocked from the outside and a balding little man wearing spectacles came in.

"See here," he demanded, "what are you men doing here? What's going on? Oh, it's you, Mr. Rarbil. Who are these men?"

Rarbil ignored the questions. "Yorty," he said, "the bank's been robbed. You go find the sheriff. And lock the door behind you. I don't want anyone coming in until the sheriff gets here."

As soon as he'd left I led Rarbil and Tomes behind the counter where Hattan was stretched out, still unconscious.

"One of you ought to see if he's all right," I said. "I found the guards hog-tied in his office. Here they are now."

Two mad and sheepish-appearing men came into the room. One of them handed me my knife.

"It was that Giucy fella. He come in with Mr. Hattan and pulled a gun on us. He made Gus, here, tie me up. Then he slugged Gus and made Mr. Hattan tie him. That's all I know. Where the hell is Hattan?"

I jerked my thumb. "On the floor over there. Giucy made him open the safe, then he slugged him. He was still out a minute ago."

At that second I felt the presence of something or someone looming over me. I looked up to see a large, fat woman with little pig eyes, a small but full-lipped rosebud of a mouth, and a triple chin.

Behind her came the voice of the fat kid, "That's him, Ma. He said he was gonna shoot me."

"Lady," I said, "you and that brat get the hell out of here before I shoot you both."

She ignored me and looked at the smaller of the two guards. "Edgar, are you going to let him talk to me like that?"

"This yer wife, Edgar?" I asked.

Edgar nodded. "Roseanne," he said, "you take the boy and go. I'll take care of things here."

She started to say something, but changed her mind. She glared at him, then glared at me and turned and left. Edgar shrugged apologetically.

"Ten years and a hundred pounds ago she was a good-lookin' woman."

Ten years and a hundred pounds. For a brief second I wondered what Esmeralda Rankin would look like ten years and a hundred pounds from now. Or Liddy, for that matter. There for a minute the idea of settling down with a woman—any woman—didn't look so good. I knowed I was no catch; I certainly wasn't no pretty boy but that didn't mean I wanted to spend the rest of my life with someone who could pass for the circus fat lady.

LeVon Tomes, who'd been tending to Chase Hattan said, "He's coming around."

At the same time the front door opened again and a man wearing a badge came in, followed by the little man with spectacles.

Kooby looked up. "Hello, Sheriff Omar. As you can see there's been a robbery here."

He nodded in my direction. "This is Del Tackett. He's working with me and my partner, Mr. Tomes here."

Clearly Rarbil felt he was taking charge. "Yorty," he said. The little man's name, I found out later, was Yorty Samms.

"Yorty, you go get a doctor for Mr. Hattan and the guard here. Tell him to bring some bandages and iodine. Sheriff, why don't we go into Hattan's office and sort out just what has happened?"

I interrupted. "Which way is Giucy likely to have went?"

The guard with the fat wife spoke up. "Closest railroad's at Pueblo, about 50 miles down the road. He gets there first and he's gone fer good."

"Kooby," I said, "you take care of things here. I'm goin' after Giucy."

He started to protest but I was already halfway out the front door. In about two seconds I was in the saddle and Old Dobbin was headed at a mile-eating canter down the road that led southeast toward Pueblo.

I'd gone about 5 miles when I drew up. It had occurred to me, how did I know Giucy was headed for Pueblo? All I had was the guard's word that that was the logical place for him to head. And all of a sudden that wasn't good enough for me. What made that guard so smart anyway? I studied on the situation for a bit, looking at all the angles. Supposing Giucy was really heading for Denver? Would we ever catch him if we all ran off to Pueblo? Not likely.

However, suppose we sent a posse on the road to Denver and another on the road to Pueblo? Some of that money was in greenbacks but a lot of it was supposed to be in gold; he'd be weighted down some so the chances were good we would catch him unless he stashed the gold somewhere, which didn't seem likely, or unless he had a hideout somewhere where even a good tracker couldn't find him and that didn't seem likely either.

But supposing, instead of running, he was to hide out right in Bonanza until things cooled off a mite. Supposing he had a friend or an accomplice in Bonanza. He could lie up there for a few days or even a few weeks and unless there was a house-to-house search, which wasn't likely either, there was no way to find him. None of us knew what his horse looked like so stabling him wouldn't be a problem. Along with all that, if he stayed hidden for a few weeks he could grow a beard or a mustache or both, lose some weight, send out for some different clothes and when he reappeared he could be somebody besides Crispen Giucy. By then, anyway, he would figure we'd given up and would feel confident to move around freely.

The more I thought about it the more it seemed to make sense that he hadn't gone anywhere. But why did that guard seem so certain he had? Was he in cahoots with Giucy? I remembered it was the other guard, not him, who Giucy slugged.

I wheeled Old Dobbin about and headed back to Bonanza. I stopped briefly at the bank but it was locked up tight with a hand-lettered sign that I studied out to read, "Closed until Tomorrow," so I went on down the road a piece until I saw a sign that said "Sheriff's Office." I tied Old Dobbin to the hitching rail in front of the office and went on in. Kooby and LeVon were inside talking to Sheriff Omar and his deputy. They looked up when I came in.

"I thought you went off to capture Crispen Giucy?" Kooby said dryly.

"Changed my mind. Got to thinkin' someone might be playin' us for suckers."

"What does that mean?" the sheriff asked.

I pulled up a straight-backed chair and sat down, straddling the seat with my arms resting on the back.

"Here's how I figure it," I said, and explained my thinking.

"Makes as much sense as runnin' off after him when you don't know what direction he went in. I was gettin' ready to send Fletch here down to Pueblo to send some wires."

"Wires?" I asked.

"Yep, to the chief of police in Denver and to lawmen all along the line from Pueblo to Abilene. It's about the best I can do right now."

"What about searchin' that guard's house?" I asked.

"What for? Because you got a wild hair ticklin' ya somewhere? That ain't good enough. I gotta have a reason—a real reason."

I started to flare back at him but Kooby held up his hand. "He's right, Tackett. You just can't go busting into a man's house without a reason. And even if there were a judge in town today I doubt very much that he would issue a search warrant just because, as the sheriff says, you have a wild hair itching you."

I changed the subject. "Where's Liddy?"

"She's up at Hattan's still. The doc took Chase home. He was in pretty bad shape—Giucy really slugged him, I guess, and Liddy said she'd look after him, at least for the rest of the day."

I turned to the sheriff. "There's three dead bodies up there and another one on the trail."

"I taken care of that," the sheriff said. "Sent a couple of men up there with a wagon. They come back just a bit ago."

I got up abruptly. "I'm goin' up to Hattan's. I don't like leavin' Liddy alone with that Mexican woman and a sick old man."

LeVon Tomes stood up. "I have to be getting back to Denver. Please say goodbye to Miss Doyle for me. I hope to see you both again."

He reached out and shook my hand. "You're a hell of a man, Del Tackett," he said.

"You're a purty good nigger, yerself," I grinned.

"And you pack a hell of a wallop," I said a few seconds later as I picked myself up off the floor and rubbed my jaw.

"Us niggers don't like you white folk calling us niggers," he said, grinning back at me.

I went outside, untied Old Dobbin and swung into the saddle. Fifteen minutes later I was knocking on the front door of Chase Hattan's place.

The door opened and I was looking into the eyes of Crispen Giucy. He had a Colt .45 in his hand and it was pointed right at my belt buckle. He had a sneering smirk on his face.

"Ah, Mr. Tackett," he said, "please come in."

He stood to one side and gestured with his pistol. As I walked by him he clubbed me on the skull with the barrel of the gun. It staggered me and I saw a bushelful of stars, but it didn't knock me down. He reached out and shoved me and I stumbled into the living room, reeled against a wall, and finally regained my balance. I shook my head to get rid of the cobwebs. As I did so, across the room I saw Liddy and a man with a bandaged head who I took to be Chase Hattan. They were sitting side by side on a sofa and a man who I recognized as the guard who'd tried to send me to Pueblo was sitting in an easy chair holding a gun on them.

I turned and looked at Giucy.

"Brave man, ain't ya," I said.

He reached out and backhanded me with his free hand, splitting my lip and drawing blood.

"We'll see how brave you are before I'm through with you," he snarled.

I could taste the blood running inside my mouth where one of my teeth had cut the inside of my lower lip. I sucked up a great gob of it and without warning spat it right at Giucy's face. He instinctively ducked back and at the same time pulled the trigger. But the wad of bloody saliva had thrown him off balance and the gun barrel swung to one side as he shot.

Even as I was reaching desperately for my gun I heard a voice say, "My God, I'm shot."

But I paid no attention to anything but hauling that gun from its holster. It came into my hand nice and smooth and all I could think of was staying alive long enough to wipe the sneer permanently off the contorted face of Crispen Giucy. As I swung the gun up level Giucy's second shot hit me in the right shoulder and my

175

shot, meant for his gut, hit him in the thigh, knocking him down to a sitting position.

My right hand all of a sudden felt weak. I couldn't raise my arm and as I tried to lift it the gun slipped from a hand that wasn't strong enough to hold it. I dived frantically after it with my left hand and palmed it as Giucy's third shot went over my head. I rolled over and flung a quick shot in his direction as his fourth one hit the floor in front of me, throwing splinters in my face. At the same time I felt a searing pain run down my chest and belly and I knew I was done for. But before I died there was one thing I had to do—kill Crispen Giucy.

Even as I thought it my gun was leveled at his face and I pulled the trigger a split second before he fired his fifth shot. My shot hit him right in the base of the neck and blew him backward so hard I heard the bump of his head hitting the floor.

Suddenly I remembered the guard with the gun and I swiveled around on the floor ready to shoot and be shot, but I didn't have to worry. He was still sitting in the chair but his gun had fallen to the floor and he was bleeding like a stuck pig.

"Don't shoot," he whispered and toppled forward out of the chair and never moved.

When I came to I was lying on the couch where Liddy and Hattan had been sitting.

The town doctor was saying, "He's lost a lot of blood but I think he'll be all right. But that bullet burn down his chest and belly is the damndest wound I ever saw. Bullet must have hit the floor and just skidded under him. Good thing it stopped when it hit his belt or it might have done some real damage."

Bleary as I was I could still see good enough to watch Liddy's face turn crimson. Even though I was hurting I heard myself chuckle a second, then I drifted out of consciousness again.

CHAPTER 16

DANG, I WAS getting tired of getting shot at and hit.

That was the conclusion I came to in the days I lay abed in Chase Hattan's big house on the mountain. And I decided it was about time I did something about it. I kept remembering Kooby Rarbil and LeVon Tomes, lawyers now because they had decided that punching cows all your life was a waste and had set out to make something of themselves. If they could do it, I could, too.

After a few days in bed I was strong enough to sit up and Liddy brought me some books from the big study that Hattan had, and I practiced up on my reading with such books as Walter Scott's *Ivanhoe*, Cooper's *The Last of the Mohicans* and Hawthorne's *The Scarlet Letter.*

By the time I'd finished *Ivanhoe* I decided it was time to try to decipher Ma's diary. She had a beautiful, educated handwriting and it was easy to tell from the way she wrote that she'd had schooling.

The diary was fragmentary, with great gaps in the later years as Ma struggled to eke out a living panning gold along the western slope of the high Sierras. But it was the beginning that I was interested in.

It turned out Ma's name before she was married was Geraldine Carmen Groupe. On her ma's side she was Irish—her ma's maiden name had been Delligan—and on her father's side she was French and Spanish. She'd been raised and gone to a girls' finishing school in Philadelphia where her father was a prosperous merchant and importer. When she was only eighteen she had met, fallen in love with, and married a dashing—at least Ma wrote that he was dashing—young army officer, Lt. Bennett William Tackett, from Virginia.

Ma had just given birth to a boy—me—when the War Between the States broke out. Lt. Ben Bill Tackett—Ma always referred to him as Ben Bill—reluctantly and painfully came to the conclusion that he would have to return home and fight for the South. When he announced his decision to Ma's parents a violent argument ensued and Ben Bill was ordered from the house.

Lacking both money and resources he had no alternative except to leave Ma and me with her parents. Before he left Philadelphia, however, he managed to get a note to her assuring her that he would come back for her after the war was over, which he thought would be only a matter of months.

He never returned. And by war's end tragedy had struck the Groupe family. Young Mrs. Tackett's parents died within a year of each other, her mother first and her father by his own hand after business reverses had left him bankrupt. For six months after the war ended Ma eked out a sparse existence, living on a small inheritance that her father had left her whilst she waited vainly for Ben Bill to return. And, after a year, she decided he was not coming back.

With a toddler to care for and no experience at making a living Ma was vulnerable to the first man to come along. He was a strapping, good-looking Union veteran named Hugh Mane who moved in on Ma with a promise of marrying her. Instead, he set out to force her to support him anyway she could. He even proposed prostitution and when she refused he beat her and threatened her child.

One night while he lay in a drunken stupor she hit him on the head with a fireplace poker, not meaning to kill him but to disable him enough to keep him from following her. Ma had hidden away a few dollars for an emergency and that night she took me and a few meager belongings and bought a train ticket to St. Louis. From there she hitched a ride on a wagon train going west, earning her way by cooking and taking turns driving a wagon which she learned to do as they crossed the plains. She dropped off in Carson City where we put up in a rooming house and she got a job as a waitress, working mostly nights whilst I slept.

That existence ended one night when a burly miner tried to attack her as she was leaving work. Now Ma, as I have said, was a big woman, nearly six feet tall, and what weight she had was mostly muscle and sinew, although it would have been hard to tell through the clothes she wore. One thing Ma had learned in her brief time with Hugh Mane was that she didn't have to put up with guff from any man and she didn't this time, either. In the struggle with the miner she was thrown to the ground where, groping desperately for some sort of a weapon, her flailing hand came across a good-sized rock. She hit the man once and then again. He gave a grunt and slumped down on top of her.

Pushing him off, she knew at once that she had killed him, so she taken off for the rooming house where we lived. Afraid the miner's friends would seek her out and either kill her or have her charged with murder, she packed up that night and fled.

A month earlier she had bought a meal for a down-on-his-luck prospector who told her he was giving up and heading back East. He said he had left his burro at a stable and if she wanted it she could have it by paying its feed bill. On impulse she had paid the bill and had taken to giving me rides on the aging animal. Now she hurried us down to the stable, tied our few belongings on the burro's back, and headed out for the Sierras, not knowing really where she was going or what her next stop would be.

When she reached the little mining camp of Lodestone she stopped to rest. And never went any farther. She found and moved into a deserted cabin, scrounged up some equipment, and went to work panning gold. Over the years, as best as I could see, she made just enough to keep us clothed and eating.

For a number of years during that period she made almost no entries in the diary except maybe to note the passing years. She never mentioned Ben Bill Tackett after she left Philadelphia. It was almost as if she had wanted to forget that part of her life. Then finally, when I was sixteen, there was one meaningful entry. It was dated May 8, 1876, and it read:

"Today I sent my beloved son Del away. It is time he went out on his own. There is nothing for him here. I pray he will find success and contentment along life's trail. If he does, perhaps one day I will see him again. If not, I pray the good Lord will care for the both of us in the years ahead and that I will see him in the far future in God's own heaven."

That was the last entry I read.

And as I read it a tear came to my eye. No one was around but I still was embarrassed. I hadn't shed a tear since I was twelve. I had thought about going back to see Ma often enough, but I never did. I was afraid if I ever went back and she saw the man I had become she would be ashamed of the big, scarred, rough-hewn wandering range hand that was her son. I had not, as she had hoped, found either success or contentment. Now, I thought that maybe, for Ma's sake, it was still not too late. I knew, anyway, that I was going to try as soon as I was able.

All the time I was recuperating, Liddy, who was staying at Hattan's to take care of the banker, who was still suffering dizzy spells from the knock on the head Giucy gave him, also was taking care of me. Over the days I was in bed she told me what had happened.

Dr. Irving, the town doctor, had brought Hattan home and after giving her instructions on caring for him, had left. A few minutes later two men in a wagon had come by and loaded the dead men in it and had gone back to town, taking with them the Mexican cook who told Liddy she was afraid to remain there and was going to stay with her daughter and son-in-law in town.

No sooner were they gone than Crispen Giucy came in through the back door, accompanied by the guard from the bank. He was in a talkative mood.

It turned out he wasn't much of a businessman and while his businesses in Abilene had prospered for awhile, by the time he'd gotten Kooby Rarbil's letter telling him he'd inherited half ownership in The Wait and See mine he was teetering on the verge of bankruptcy and it was plain that he could not be reelected to the city council.

When he'd learned that Liddy had inherited the other half of the mine and the $50,000 he set out to marry her. When she turned him down he decided to take by force what he couldn't gain by guile. He'd hired Dot Matricks to make sure neither Liddy nor I got to Denver, but at that time he wasn't ready to have Liddy killed because he knew he would be the chief suspect. But anyone else was fair game. So Dot Matricks killed Morgan Adams in order to get Liddy away from him and tried to kill me. After all, I was only a wandering cowboy who no one would ever miss.

When Giucy had found himself on the same train with Ada Venn he put two and two together and decided, wrongly, that she was going to Denver on Liddy's behalf, so he killed her and threw her body off the train, thinking it would be weeks or months before it was found. When he found the papers Ada had stolen from Liddy it convinced him even more that she was going to Denver on Liddy's behalf.

"I never told him differently," Liddy said. "Ada was desperate or she'd have never done what she did."

Greasy-Hair—I never did learn his name, the two blond gunmen, and Phil Kimby had all been on Giucy's payroll in Abilene. When he arrived in Bonanza he discovered that one of the guards had once worked for him, and after he discovered that his half ownership in The Wait and See was worthless, he quickly bribed the man to help in the robbery attempt.

He'd initially thought to hide out in the guard's house but the fat woman and her fat brat were more than he could put up with so he decided to take over Hattan's place because, he figured, no one would look for him there.

And maybe he was right. When I went up there it wasn't because I thought he'd be there, it was just that I was uneasy about leaving Liddy alone with a sick man.

Well, she was still alone and caring for two sick men—me and old Chase Hattan—but with Giucy and his gunmen all dead there didn't seem to be much to worry about. Besides Kooby Rarbil was hanging around. He claimed to have more business in Bonanza but I noticed he found a lot of time to be at Hattan's. And it was clear Liddy had taken a shine to him, too.

I had mixed feelings about that. I liked her fussing over me and I was just a little jealous when her and Kooby began making eyes at each other, but I had to admit that I had no claim on her. Not only that but there was a girl waiting for me back at the R Bar R if I was ever smart enough to return.

By the middle of the third week I was up and walking around and by the end of the fourth week I decided it was time for me to hit the road. My shoulder was still stiff but I could use my right hand pretty good. The main thing bothering me was the constant itch along the red scar that ran from the top of my chest clean down to my navel. But that was not enough to keep me from going.

I borrowed two more books from Hattan, *The Decline and Fall of the Roman Empire* by Gibbon and a book called *Pride and Prejudice* by a lady named Jane Austen. I packed them in a saddlebag along with Ma's diary and said my goodbyes to Hattan and Liddy and

Kooby, who, as usual, was visiting. Liddy thanked me "for every-thing you've done for me."

"I'll never be able to repay you," she said. "Can't you stay a little longer?"

It all sounded nice but if I'd stayed a little longer I would have just been in her and Kooby's way. So I shook hands all around and climbed on Old Dobbin and we went down the road toward Bonanza. I figured to spend a couple of days there, outfit myself, and then head out for the Arizona territory. Maybe even go by the R Bar R, if I could manage to get the picture of that fat woman out of my mind and what the guard had said about her being a beauty ten years earlier.

I rode into Bonanza and pulled up in front of the Bonanza Hotel. I was signing my name on the register when a woman's voice at my shoulder said, "Welcome to Bonanza, Mr. Tackett."

I turned around and stared. It was Dot Matricks. Her busted wrist was still in a sling but otherwise she looked perky enough.

Quick-like I stepped back out of her reach. "I thought you was in jail," I said.

"Just briefly," she said. "They really didn't have any proof I'd done anything wrong so they had to let me go. I came here to collect what Mr. Giucy owed me but they tell me you killed him, so I've been waiting for you. Can we go somewhere and talk?"

"Lady," I said, "I don't want to get anywhere near ya."

"Oh come now," she said. "If I'd wanted to kill you I could have done it just now when your back was turned."

"What is it ya want?"

"I need a stake to get back to Kansas City."

"Lady," I said, "you can walk to Kansas City for all of me."

I had turned and started for the stairway when I thought I heard the whisper of a sound behind me. I threw myself onto the floor rolling to one side as I did so. In her rush to get at me Dot Matricks couldn't stop. I felt her shoe kick the side of my leg and looked up in time to see her stagger and stumble to the floor.

Then she screamed and as I crawled around to look at her I could see why. The hat pin she had meant for my back was sticking deep into the palm of her hand. As I watched, her eyes rolled into the back of their sockets, her face contorted, and she gave a deep shudder and then lay still. I was standing looking down at her when the desk clerk came running from a back room.

"What happened?" he asked, all out of breath.

"Danged if I know," I said. "I seen her stumble and fall. That's all I know. Must have had a seizure or somethin'."

I turned and headed for the door. To heck with hanging around Bonanza. Today was as good a day as any to head for Arizona and check and see if a dark-haired girl named Esme was as slender and pretty as I remembered.

Coming Soon

TACKETT

&

THE SALOON KEEPER

TACKETT
3
TRILOGY